dead ink

– Liverpool –
MMXXIV

A
SCARAB
WHERE
THE
HEART
SHOULD
BE

dead ink

First published in Great Britain in 2024 by Dead Ink,
an imprint of Cinder House Publishing Limited.

Print ISBN 9781915368614
eBook ISBN 9781915368621

Cover design by Luke Bird / lukebird.co.uk
Typeset by Laura Jones-Rivera / lauraflojo.com
Editing by Jack Ramm / Rammstudios.co.uk

Printed and bound in Great Britain
by Clays Ltd, Elcograf S.p.A.

www.deadinkbooks.com

Supported using public funding by
ARTS COUNCIL
ENGLAND

Funded by
UK Government

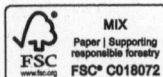

MIX
Paper | Supporting
responsible forestry
FSC® C018072

A SCARAB WHERE THE HEART SHOULD BE

Marieke Bigg

dead ink

A
SCARAB
WHERE
THE
HEART
SHOULD
BE

Marieke Bigg

dead ink

To Bruce

'As I lie in bed I assume
the shape of a big beetle,
a stag beetle or a cockchafer,
I think.'
– Franz Kafka,
Wedding Preparations in the Country

We turn the page of our newspaper's cultural supplement and find a picture of a house. A flat and lonesome cube, comprised of three chambers, one below and two above, made entirely of glass. It is warm outside, we can see. The house hovers over a sun-blanched pasture. It is imposing and expensive, alien amidst the raw and rusty grass. The ground is charged, we sense, with the fever of insects in the hay. Late summer abounds, and yet, the house itself looks dead.

A figure stands in the eerie glow of the kitchen, a slender shadow of a woman,

one hand resting on an empty cooking island, she gazes past the camera, through the reflective sheath of the house's walls. And while we know that out there the pasture is brimming with life, something about the glaze of her vacant eyeballs makes us certain that all she sees is black.

We wonder why she has put herself there. Why she has chosen to put the intimacies of every egg boiled in the kitchen, every night slept in the bed, and every moment of nothingness so relentlessly on display. Something about the angle of her body, fractionally turned away, a light shadow cast across her face by the half-curtain of a fringe, makes us feel we are intruding, that we have breached her privacy. That what she really wants is for us to look away.

She is so lonely, we think.

Just then, the hairs in our ear canals twitch with an unearthly pitch, a shriek that spans the air, as taut as the glass of the walls. A sound akin to a dying breath. We grasp at our chests, checking for the life inside our own cavity. And now we're aching for someone to hold, close and tight. We need to feel the fleshiness of another pulse. Because something about looking at Jacky Mackenzie in her award-winning marvel of modern architecture is like being confronted with the terror of losing everything we once loved. We catch our breath and take in the shiny promise of a picture. Then we turn away.

PART 1

LINES

1

They wanted it to be like Johnson's glass house. That corner-stone of high-modernist architecture; a house entirely transparent. They loved it for the reasons other people didn't. Because it subordinated human comforts to a vision.

His arms were wrapped tight around her the day they watched the first glass wall go up.

'We'll be like fish in an aquarium,' he said.

'I prefer plants in a greenhouse.' Jacky looked down at the tendrils of his arms: his hands clasped together over the space around her bellybutton like a thick knot of roots. She considered the possibility for a moment that they might be more conventional than they thought, that the next step in their relationship could also be the sprouting of new life.

'Why plants?' He asked her, nestling his stubbled chin deeper into the nape of her neck.

'Plants are perfect designs.' She turned her head to catch his gaze, to see if he understood. 'They're perfectly functional. They're implicitly indispensable. They have made themselves necessary in their ecosystem.'

Mark nodded but didn't respond. He never really engaged with her architectonics. Sometimes she thought that he might be intimidated by her aptitude for concepts; most people were. But that didn't matter, he listened in his own way, making himself permeable to her.

It was enough just to feel his breath on her neck.

Besides, she already knew what he heard. Freedom. That word was how he sold their buildings. Mark recognised simple truths, knew how to distil Jacky's grandiosity into human emotion. He translated her message into something relatable and, in doing so, had introduced to Jacky the possibility that she might be human too. With the vines of his arms holding her, she felt like people might finally accept her.

'They're so perfect, we often don't notice them. Only when we put them in a vase, do we appreciate their melding of form and function. Although, of course, most people don't realise that's what they're looking at. They just call it 'beauty'.' She scoffed, then, out of habit. Briefly breaking with the serenity of their moment.

'Good buildings are vases. They draw attention to the spaces they contain. We don't impose design on nature, only draw attention to its already perfect architecture. That's all we need to do.'

Mark spun Jacky around and kissed her, the way he always did when she got close to lyrical (close is the furthest she'd ever get).

In a way, Mark did for Jacky what Jacky did for the world. He held the space for her to grow. And Jacky did the same for him, fuelling his marketing brain with new designs and visions. That was their relationship's structural mechanism.

'We're just custodians of nature. People will remember that when they see us in here.'

They'd built their castle in East Sussex. Remote, or as remote as was viable – removed from the broil of the city, but close enough for meetings with clients. This was where the glass house was supposed to live. Surrounded by the deep damp green, its elegant flatness was a privileged platform for taking in the isolation their hard-earned labours had bought. Surrounded by glass walls, they were immersed in, though not physically subjected to, the awesome might of the great outdoors.

That suited them well.

Jacky and Mark had long ago decided to translate their architectural principles to their relationship; to unite the personal and professional in one seamless structure. *Stream-lining*, they called it.

'People are trapped. We'll show them how to live,' they'd muttered to each other back at architecture school; uncannily aligned in matters of head and heart.

Together, they'd decided to do away with drab walls and relationship conventions. They'd love each other but they wouldn't always live together. They'd travel around, have their own lives. Spread themselves and their spores; they wouldn't be sexually exclusive. They'd do away with emotional clutter like jealousy. They didn't need it. They just needed wide open, intentional space. They'd live in the airiest of constructions, allowing their natural ambition to thrive. Together, they'd transcend the petty, fleshy needs that stifled most people, that imprisoned them inside the dull shapes of solid brick and mortar silos.

Streamlining, they called it. And it had worked. Their elegant philosophy had sprouted an award-winning firm, iconic buildings, and years of productive collaboration. It had removed the incongruencies most people felt when they moved between the realms of work and home, from public to private. All these fragmented versions of themselves, none of them satisfying, because they didn't twine into a coherent whole. Mark and Jacky shared a direction, and so they wasted no time. They flowed towards greatness.

Streamlining had brought them here, to the threshold of their constitution. Now they were impregnable. Who could break emptiness? End the unending? Dismantle the void? This building was unbreakable, and so was their partnership, because both were largely empty space.

2

The day Jacky met Mark wasn't about him. She was fleshier back then, her figure more conventionally feminine, but she was still not enough of a woman to cast herself in a romance. Back then, at the beginning of her training, she already knew how to slice through the day unhindered by personal relationships. Sharp, focused, on guard, she entered the department. Pencils sharpened, ready to slip past the other students to the front of the room. Ready to work harder than any of them, to leave them trembling in her wake.

Her unrivalled efforts had left her ostracised. Faces turned away as she walked down the central aisle of the classroom. *Progress depends on isolation*, she told herself. But it also depended on a work bench. Just a few months into her undergraduate degree in architecture, no one wanted to share a space with her.

She scowled at the human-sized children, who had wandered cluelessly into a field they knew nothing about. Among them, Mark hadn't impressed her particularly. Not with his chiselled jawline. Nor his easy charm. Only, he had at least been discernible from the homogenous crowd. There was a smell about him that made him distinctive and relatable. Sweat.

Mark talked to people but he kept them at arm's length. That made her trust him. It let her lock eyes with him that morning that wasn't about him.

'Later than usual,' he'd said, face turned to her like a heart-shaped moon, so clear and bright she could almost see her reflection in it.

Jacky had said nothing. Mark had disorientated her. She put her thermos down on the far-right hand corner of the bench, arranged papers and equipment, clutching for control, as her left side tingled with the charge of his body next to hers.

She felt hot and trapped between the angles of her pencils, rulers, and the many eyes on her. They were all watching, she knew. They were the kind of people who watched; she and Mark were the kind of people they looked at.

'I was working on something.' She finally managed to say. And he made her tell him everything.

It took Jacky some time to let Mark into her picture. At first, she lacked the conceptual toolkit to make sense of teamwork. It didn't happen overnight, but it did happen by the light of his moon-face. It felt good to see her ideas illuminated by his dimpled blue. Watching them turn from good to celestial. She got used to having him there, until she needed him there, until she couldn't execute a single vision, compose a single design, without holding them up to him. He never had an opinion. He didn't need to do anything, say anything, he just needed to not resist. She trusted him to stop her from straying off course, that was his function. Less inspiration than security. Then a dependency. Over time, she forgot that he was the moon, and she the sun.

He showed her a different kind of beauty. Architecture had always been about aesthetics to her, the patterns and cadences of form that made a beautiful sense to her. But Mark showed her something else, something silkier. The beauty of *the idea* of doing something. How you could romanticize architecture and idolise the role of the architect. How you could make a performance of that love affair, indulge in it. How that made a personal relationship, one you could communicate and share.

After they graduated, they worked together from a makeshift office at the back of the architecture school. The housekeeper let them use the shed after-hours. He'd agreed after they'd caught him scoffing the remnants of Adderall the students left in their lockers. He told them they were diehards because they never stopped working. He'd stand across from them, staring into the space between them, as they stood side by side. He'd tell them he knew who the real winners were, the black holes of his pupils showing them their potential.

After their days in the shed, they'd bar-hop around Soho, drawing ideas on the backs of coasters. Mark always had sheets of cardboard in his tote bag that he'd pull out when he saw a building he liked, folding them to make a replica. That's how he taught her to move away from her desk and out of her thoughts. To sink into the unfamiliar space within her body, and to let others' visions move her. He showed her in that small way, that she could be less alone. It was the most generous thing he would ever do.

Back then, they were hungry, greedy. No building defied comprehension. Every renovated warehouse, every terraced cottage, annexed semi-detached or multi-story skyrise; all were reducible to cardboard creased in the right places, to crumpled paper in the palms of their hands. Looking down at the structures that held families and couples and cosy people, they never envied the lives they contained. They knew that there was nothing to it, just an illusion. Just the same walls framing the self-same emptiness in a different configuration. They would not be seduced by the allures of captivity – there were other, more inspired ways to be alone, together.

3

Jacky did not have any trouble settling into the house. The glass prism fit her perfectly. She didn't move in; she *slipped* into it. Seamlessly, she let herself be enveloped by the new and perfect sheen. The glass that surrounded her only set her free. She always knew it would. These were the conditions she needed to grow.

Here, her chest burst open like an estuary. The frantic murmur of her overworked heart slowed to a steady hum. She sighed the trapped breath of a lifetime. She was finally home. She bathed in that openness. She luxuriated in it. She curled up for afternoons in the dappled puddles of light that gathered around her like leaves on a forest floor. She nestled in that warmth, petrichor replaced by the fresh smell of laser-cut shards and wooden beams. By the deliberate, seamless production of a house in her own vision. She spent hours on her side, inches from a glass pane, looking into its refractions. She'd never been so still.

She didn't take notice of Mark as he hovered anxiously in some square of dead space. He'd have his reward, she thought, when the pictures of the house came, when the PR buzz took hold and he got to talk. But *this*, this was Jacky's moment.

Mark struggled to take the same view.

'What are you doing?'

She smiled at him, mouth wide and child-like.

'I told you.'

She stared at him, waiting for him to catch up. He looked agitated – vibrating, almost, as he shifted his weight between his feet. Too much caffeine, perhaps, although the real problem was that he seemed to have lost touch with the whole purpose of their operation.

'I told you. This house is a greenhouse. It's a place for growth.'

He sighed, and checked his watch, looked around the room, eyes searching for another coffee. Anything to fuel his anxiety, it seemed.

'Seeds germinate in frost. This is my winter. I look still, but I'm in the process of sprouting new life.'

He stared at her.

'You're burnt out,' he said. 'You should see someone.'

But Jacky felt better than ever. Despite her lifelong commitment to her vision, all the prize-winning buildings and endless new clients, she'd never truly believed them until now. Lying here, at peace with herself, she had all the validation she needed.

It made sense that this wasn't enough for Mark. While they'd shared the same structural metaphors for love and life, their motivations had always differed. Jacky wanted transcendence; Mark wanted success. Until now, their difference had sustained them. Their distinct orientations had complemented each other perfectly. Jacky's insatiable drive to birth herself through her structures were the engine of the operation; Mark's business acumen the enabler. Jacky thrived in the company of her own ideas; Mark liked to exercise his charms on other people.

For all the work Jacky put into each and every one of their commissions, everything until now, really, had been Mark's terrain. It had all been public-facing: networking, clients, countless stylistic compromises. They'd been operating in his comfort zone. Jacky made concessions pragmatically, but also painfully, to accommodate the firm's needs. This was her pocket of time and light. She needed it to return to herself.

It was disconcerting that Mark didn't trust her process just as, for the first time in her life, Jacky fully trusted herself. Now that she trusted her body to rest and restore her to action when the time was right, trusted her own regenerative potential. Now that they lived in Jacky's comfort zone. Perhaps Mark was threatened by her sudden total independence. It didn't take him long to drag them back into familiar territory. He let the weekend pass before he darted for the office. He returned in the evening, armed with the first review.

'Have you been here all day?'

Jacky did not turn to him from her spot by the window, sensing what was coming, like a plant senses the setting sun.

'This is important,' he said, pulling the knitted blanket she'd draped over herself at dusk from her body. She rolled from her side onto her back and looked up at him.

'They're starting to turn on us. Journalists don't take rejection well. They're starting to say you're indifferent.'

Jacky stared up a while longer, trying to understand why he couldn't let her have her peace.

'What's new.' She rolled back onto her side. She knew what they were saying. They weren't the first to have said it: she'd faced critics at every stage of her career, and, if she was honest, in her life before architecture too. She had a way of irritating people: they called it arrogance, but what they were talking about was passion; her devotion to patterns over people.

'This is important.'

She said nothing. She didn't respond to manipulation. He was trying to scare her back into motion. PR was *his* responsibility.

Then he threw her a copy of a newspaper. He didn't try to soften the blow, just tossed the explosive at her. Jacky watched the wad of cellulose land. His tactics were working, he was starting to drag her out of her newfound sense of natural potential, but part of her still expected the paper to burst into a blossom, or a tree.

'Turn to the Culture section.'

Jacky heaved herself up to sitting and turned the pages, slowly. The raw of her fingertips against the grainy paper reminded her how she'd earned the right to rest.

She scanned the page. Jacky wasn't unaccustomed to finding herself reproduced in pixels and ink. She'd been reviewed plenty of times over the years. But previous replications had focused on her buildings, and been restricted to the pages of specialist magazines. A blown up shot of herself in a national newspaper was different.

The photo appeared alongside one of the house, with Jacky in it. Still fully dressed, thank God. If they'd come the next day, they would have found her stripped down to her underwear in her process of basking. She hadn't invited a photographer, and so it was disconcerting to think that a journalist had snapped the shot without her knowing it. That they had shown up, at dusk, Jacky inferred, from the angle of the shadows (angles were, after all, Jacky's particular expertise), from a position just fractionally off centre, from their front lawn. How had she missed it? It annoyed Jacky to think that the city had followed them. But it was more than that. If she was honest, the thought of being alone and exposed to the judgements of the humans she thought to have finally escaped, terrified her.

All this was before she read on.

After a perfunctory and, in Jacky's view, hugely reductive account of her design portfolio, the journalist of the article went on to describe, with reference to the accompanying photograph, a vague resemblance between the contours of Jacky's previous designs, and Jacky's silhouette. In the photo, Jacky appeared in her usual style of dress. Bulbous black silhouettes pinched into a tip-like shape of a wing; her short, black hair, sleeked back into the same pointed teardrop shape; her thick-rimmed glasses like bulging beetle's eyes. Based on her shape in the photograph and a few de-contextualised, slightly curt remarks the journalist had haphazardly collected from a range of interviews with former classmates and clients, they had found, apparently, sufficient evidence to deduce a pattern of behaviour to dub Jacky, 'The Beetle'.

The nickname was superficially comical but had a dark underbelly, given that this had not been the first time Jacky had been accused of cold-blooded ruthlessness. And it stung, at first.

Jacky looked up at Mark for the moral support she'd come to expect of him. The way he used to with their classmate's digs. Back then, he knew exactly how to soothe her. Moving in close but never overtly comforting her. Making himself an invisible crutch, an empowering bolster. That day, though, he only loomed over her, tall and unrelenting.

'Why are you showing me this?'

His eyes a ruthless black, like beetle skin. They pinned her to the floor.

'This is your problem, Mark.'

He stared at her a while longer.

'I know it is.'

She looked up at him, surprising herself by feeling slightly intimidated. He had caught her in an uncharacteristically vulnerable state after all.

'OK, so sort it.'

He remained hovering a while longer, still silent.

'I fully intend to.'

Jacky sighed. His overblown performance had suddenly lost its charge. She got up.

'So, get to it.'

Her joints creaked as she stretched her legs for the first time that day, and turned to walk away.

'I need you to do an interview.'

Part of his barrage. Jacky stopped.

'I won't do it.'

'You have to.'

'We have an agreement, Mark. You're front-of-house.'

He flinched.

'Yes, well, that was until you revealed your star potential.'

'You're not jealous, are you?'

The voids of his pupils had narrowed into petty slits. It made him unattractive. Jacky wanted to tell him. But she contained herself, she always did. Her silence on certain matters was integral to their structure. Like the fact that he enjoyed managing the sea of people who hated her, because it boosted his own popularity. Like the fact that being her human face was foundational to his ego.

'I'm asking you to do this for the firm.' He stopped and his eyes scanned Jacky's near-naked body. 'Besides, it might be good for you. Some re-socialising.'

That comment did strange things to her. She wanted to throw herself at him. She imagined slamming her fists against his chest, then clutching his body between her thighs. She imagined their vines entangled on the floor of her greenhouse. A decade ago, perhaps she would have done it. Now, intimacy seemed a tad too visceral. The space between them had widened. And they had to let it be. That was their agreement. Jacky still valued their agreements even if Mark no longer did. Because she valued the natural laws they'd based them on.

VERSES ON ENTOMOLOGY

Rosemary Beetle
Chrysolina americana
6-8mm

The rosemary beetle poses a challenge to the human hierarchy of values. Beautiful, and exotic adventurers, they arrived in Britain in the mid-1990s, most likely on the back of rosemary plant. With metallic green and purple stripes, they populate rosemary and other aromatic plants, including lavender, sage and thyme. Gardeners watch the delightful bug gnaw at the corners of their beloved and most fragrant plants and have a decision to make: to prioritise their aesthetic pleasure from beetle or plant. That choice will determine whether the beetle is cast as a pest or a treasure. Arbitrary distinctions based on human whims.

Of course, we know where their instincts will take them – to the unthreatening stillness of the plants. The beetle's oily stripes too closely resemble the flag of a claim to coexistence in the perfectly civilised garden.

People bring the same fickle fancy to their evaluations of the human species, as they decide what to think of people. To let them live in the gardens they make, or to annihilate them. To choose peace or power. It isn't a well-considered decision. The outcome doesn't matter to them. They're just playing games. To pass the time.

4

Jacky MacKenzie had woken up one day to discover she was a beetle.

She'd decided to approach the whole thing with curiosity. There was Jacky and there was The Beetle. She'd always been a pragmatist when it came to matters of identity. She considered herself a postmodernist in that very particular sense. She was happy to let people decide her meaning, happy for multiple versions of herself to coexist. She'd always survived that way. When it came to people's judgements, she had learnt to inhabit the space between her self-perception and the outlandish versions mirrored back at her. She had learned to inspect them, with the attentiveness of the entomologist. To categorize them in order to operationalise them. Dividing herself into the taxonomy of species she needed to distance herself from people's judgements. On the surface, it seemed alienating. But these imperfect replications meant that Jacky's true meaning survived. New guises, new skins; all translations of the streamlining, all towards the same end. She could let herself be the bitch, or the recluse or the maverick. It all came very naturally to a woman who had always defined herself by her output. Who had always experienced herself as a void.

It wouldn't be a straightforward process, not an instantaneous metamorphosis like Kafka's bureaucrat. But, if Mark wanted her to do an interview, so be it. Like everything, she would simply make it an exercise in marrying form and function.

The pieces were already there, of course, the natural elements that were always the building blocks. Her life already tended towards the streamline paddle of a beetle's back. There was truth in every perspective. What the journalist had picked up on was, in actual fact, a cohesiveness that connected her designs to her lifestyle choices. A style of *being*. To the journalist, it was disconcerting, the way she trimmed the unnecessary fat from her life. That was streamlining. Not cold; just consistent. Jacky realised that she needed to explain it to them. How the aerodynamic shapes of her designs were streamlined. How her suits were streamlined. How her hair was streamlined. How she drank her espressos black because it was streamlined. How she and Mark adhered to a strict paleo diet that did away with the artificial rituals people had imposed on eating. None of the heat and steam convoluting dinner. Just cold lean strips of efficiency. When journalists asked her in interviews why she'd never had children, she'd tell them that her ovaries were streamlined too.

What this journalist had given her, was a gift, an invitation towards greater consistency.

5

Clarissa first read about The Beetle with a shudder of fore-boding. Jacky had been on this course for a while, but Clarissa had clung to the hope of redirecting her.

She'd first seen Jacky sitting on the pier in Brighton, a slither of a silhouette like the black outline of the seagulls on the horizon. She walked closer and saw the colour of her face, the grey of unfulfilled love, and she knew she could tell her anything. It was safe because she could see that Jacky wouldn't try to protect her, or to make her dreams come true.

That's how it was between them, in the early days – Jacky always showing only a slice of herself. It was very generous, Clarissa had thought at first, for someone to take up so little space, to give so much of it to another. That's before she'd understood how much work it would be to fill in the blanks.

Clarissa sat her strong, broad body down on the wood next to Jacky's wavering frame. She'd never seen someone both so unbearably fragile and undeniably commanding. She wanted to protect her and throw herself at her feet simulta-neously. Neither of those impulses were ever fully satisfied, although both came to consume her.

'You don't look like you belong here,' she'd said, realising immediately how ridiculous that comment sounded in a Canadian accent.

Jacky had barely looked at her, head still half-tilted towards the ocean, the white shine of cloudy light blotting out the missing half, so that she looked like an elongated figure in a Picasso painting – a fragmented sculpture of shadow and light. A disassembled woman. Both everything and nothing at once.

'I don't really belong anywhere,' she eventually answered.

Clarissa felt the wavering haziness of the words flitter towards her. Their sadness, their decay. And she knew that, just like her, Jacky was a woman determined to disappear. Together, Clarissa thought, even back then, maybe they could find the conditions in which they'd want to be seen.

Clarissa had missed out on dating at high-school for obvious reasons. A small town in the least progressive of Canada's backwaters wasn't a place to experiment. But it wasn't her sexuality that had made her leave a place that had never felt like home. To strangers, she'd say it was that culture of Canadian openness that made her run. Always eager, helpful neighbours, always performed joviality that wanted you to disappear into a stereotype. She wanted the cool distance of the Brits, an attitude that would let her do her thing. She said. Disinterest was the closest to acceptance she could imagine. In her life, in her relationships, this was freedom.

She only told her therapist the truth.

And the whales.

The whales had found her, not the other way round. Life told you what you needed to hear. She'd always believed that.

It was the reason she didn't engage in the gossip in the coffee breaks at the hospital. She detached herself from the babble, didn't let it suck her in. Truths found you eventually, however inconvenient.

The whales had found her at night. In the glimmer of the ocean cast in the white light of a laptop screen, they beckoned to her on OrcaCam.

She needed them when her shifts ended. After the shitstorms of the twenty-four--hour days of her medical training. She'd arrive home at the crack of dawn, skulking up the stairs of her parents' house to her childhood bedroom. Still stuck living at home at thirty, not really because money was tight but because it didn't really matter where she lived, because she wasn't living. She'd get home, open up her laptop and gaze into the pixelated grey, waiting for something unexpected to rear its head.

She learnt quickly, could tell her Blue from her Bowhead and her Grey. There was something about categorisation that made her look closer. A kind of expansive refinement. Like quantum explosion, the closer she looked, the bigger her world became. It was similar to learning anatomy but somehow more powerful. How you needed that attention to detail to properly appreciate even the world's largest mammals.

They found her, too, the night her life swallowed her up.

She'd been toughing out a particularly painful stint in the urology clinic. Her placement was supposed to be coming to an end. She'd been promised a better one that aligned with her interests, in cardiology. It wasn't like the choice was between dicks and hearts, it wasn't that poetic. Although there was one particular dick she had been trying to escape. A supervisor who'd made the experience of inspecting phalluses protruding through holes in green surgical sheets as creepy as you'd imagine it to be. Dr Savart was the perverted doctor you'd like to dismiss as a juvenile joke. Who took sexual delight in taking trainees of the female variety under his wing, and training them up to revere the male appendage. Clarissa had hoped that her square body would make him forget she was a woman. It didn't, of course; somehow men always find a way to remember. All it did was make him both disdainful *and* less accommodating. The continual backhanded compliments about her shape, temperament, abilities. 'None of this will phase you, you're built like a warrior'. Weird comments that made her grateful that he'd chosen, at least, to make male anatomy the flesh he'd physically cut into. And at the same time, it made her wonder, in her most despondent moments, about the shady figures lurking in gynaecology.

Freedom is in the details, she told herself while hovering over specimens and under Dr Savart's disgusting gaze. Just focus on the problem at hand; look closely enough, at the twist or scar or lesion and it's no longer a penis, but a mechanism in need of repair. Look closely enough, and you forget about the people turning problems of functionality into power games.

She'd always expected Dr Savart to be the man-sized barricade to her career progression, but it turned out to be Dr Ferrara in cardiology who blindsided her by choosing another applicant for the position. It was totally unexpected. It took her a while to understand what had happened.

But the truth had found her, as it always did. It had cut through over instant coffee on a night shift, white coats on the other side of the room forming judgements in a huddle.

A sad sentence had darted towards her, splicing her in two. One half of her was angry at Dr Ferrara. The other half, although she hated to admit it, was angry at the woman who had slept with him for the position.

She went home on the familiar seesaw of sleeplessness and caffeine undulations with an unfamiliar sense of utter despair. Back to the whales, to pretend that she was riding that wave, not drowning in it.

Back to her childhood bedroom. To that other pole in the strange oscillation her life had become; between the profanity of penises and the regression of her childhood bedroom. To the absurdity of this twisted, lesbian form of a Freudian quip.

Freedom is in the details, she muttered to herself that night. She'd just mistaken the cusp of a wave for the edge of a Humpback's tail. The words came drifting back to her, from across the shore, from her mother's lips.

Sitting in her childhood bedroom, she heard them for the first time. That singsong she'd grown up with at breakfast. The chorus her mother clung to as she folded napkins and arranged forks like her life depended on it. She wasn't angry with her mother. Not like her friends who, caught in the trappings of cis femininity, had to reject their mother's traditionalism to find themselves. Clarissa was nothing like her mother, that was a given. Her struggles and her answers had nothing to do with the family. They were social problems. Of discrimination. They had nothing to do with her mother.

Is there anything more magnificent than a whale's breach? Water cascading down its hefty flanks, a fountain of supernatural force, pure bulk defying gravity's laws?

Clarissa swivelled around in her desk chair. She took in her childhood bedroom. No longer a child but what was she? A sad woman growing older in secret. She was trapped in her sense of her own otherness. She'd insisted she was different for so long but she didn't know who she was.

She had never gone to see the whales in person.

Life was so far away. And so she'd moved towards it. Looking for the courage to let it change her.

Dr Savant didn't care she was leaving. Ferrara probably never heard. Her colleagues undoubtedly speculated about her reasons. She decided they'd be the last people she'd leave behind knowing so little about her.

Clarissa had moved far away, but she'd done it to get closer to people. She wanted to do more than inspect earholes and buttholes and physical wounds. She wanted to sink her teeth into the human condition, to feel the kind of connection that risked it all. She became a therapist. Overall, she was happier. At least, it was a step in the right direction. And when she first saw that cipher of a woman on the pier, she thought it was another truth coming to her.

Only Jacky resisted meaning. And Clarissa found herself at that familiar safe distance she'd wanted to leave behind. She accepted it too easily. Occasionally she'd try to ask for more, but not really. It was easier to wait for Jacky to come to her. To exist in that liminal space, pretending to be in an intimate relationship, against the ever-receding horizon of their real commitment.

But that newspaper article was another graze with reality. A barely-there touch, but she couldn't unfeel it. Clarissa knew her lover. Her self-destructive tendencies. How she sacri-ficed everything to the fleeting illusion of a personal victory. She knew that she'd see the article as a challenge. And that she never saw that she had anything to lose. Clarissa knew her lover like she knew herself. And her reticent hope that their two negatives would make a positive, reared its head and wailed.

VERSES ON ENTOMOLOGY

Swollen-thighed beetle
Oedemera nobilis
6-11mm

Like many beetles, *Oedemera nobilis* are excellent pollinators. But despite their considerable public service, these particular specimens need to be appreciated primarily for their style.

They sport large emerald bulges on their thighs that bellow out like statement trouser legs. Their other wiry extensions, are the elegant wisps on the end of a cursive script. They are integrally stylish. Exemplars of adaptive pizazz.

Even their place of work mirrors their fabulousness. Their productive hours are spent inside statement blooms. Poppies, roses, or daisies. From within these large, open flowers, they shine like the jewels they were meant to be.

Although fierce and singular, she needs the right conditions to grow.

Not just harmless, but essential, they sustain the ecosystem we all depend on. Integral to the web of life that holds us, and yet, humans have found ways to absolve themselves of gratitude. They feast their eyes and stomachs on nature's abundance. But they don't think about those who work tirelessly in the under-growth. The beetles who give them suste-nance and inspiration. The architects who give them shelter and inspiration.

Without a thought to their dependency.

The beetle doesn't need recognition, she is happy to be left to work. Her gratification comes from the doing. *But she would prefer not to be vilified.*

6

The journalist arrived at the house at 11am. The time had been agreed between her and Mark, although Mark made himself scarce for the interview. A convenient meeting had called him to Sweden, which is where he'd fled increasingly over the past years, although he worked hard to make it seem less like fleeing. Nordic countries were at the forefront of progressive everything, he kept telling her in that publicity drawl he didn't seem to be able to switch off. Eventually he bought an apartment in Stockholm.

From her glass pedestal, she could see the journalist's car bumbling down the country roads from a mile away; she'd been especially vigilant since the surprise photograph. That gave her plenty of time to fidget and pace. Although she did everything she could to pretend she wasn't nervous. Glancing at sketches, pretending to read emails. Eventually she gave up. It felt blasphemous, voiding work of its meaning like that.

Instead, Jacky stood in the doorway straightening her clothes and practicing her smile. Mark had told her repeatedly to be 'nice' to the journalist. Mocking her in her misery. It was perverse, in fact, the more she thought about it. Everything they'd done was a direct consequence of everything she was. Now he was trying to change her. It was ungrateful, and unsustainable. He'd soon realise that nothing held when she wasn't in her strength.

The journalist was suddenly much closer. Her figure had appeared at the end of the driveway. Jacky shook herself into the present. She worked on inverting the downcast corners of her mouth. Thinking of her face as a set of planes made the whole façade feel less disingenuous.

The journalist arrived at the door. Too soon. Jacky was still easing into her new emotional posture. They stared at each other through the glass door. For a moment, it was like looking into a mirror. Jacky was struck by the uncanny resemblance between herself and the journalist. Not a product of narcissism, as she knew Mark would have said. It was undeniable. She was broader, stronger (most people were), but her hair, the androgenous angle of her jaw, the sad depression of her eyelids, a mole in exactly the same place on her left cheek. The journalist stared back with none of Jacky's surprise, just, perhaps, a tinge of discomfort. *Good*, Jacky thought, *let's rebalance the scales*. The journalist had come armed with foresight. She'd had the time to process her similarity to the outlandish woman she'd seen in the newspaper. Perhaps her colleagues had teased her about it, and maybe she'd lashed back, telling them not to be unprofessional. Terrified that they'd landed on something. Perhaps she'd come to the interview guarded, determined not to find any similarity between herself and The Beetle. Most people did.

Jacky opened the door and flashed a smile, already sensing it was a lost cause. Sometimes, Mark had told her, it was worse when she tried. It just came across bitchy. Those cutting comments used to be softened by the guiding principles he gave her. 'You're best when you're focused, when you're not trying to be someone,' he used to say. Jacky's stomach cramped into something reminiscent of sadness at the kindness he could have shown her only a few weeks ago.

'Would you like a coffee?' Jacky shuddered at the chill in her own voice.

The woman looked at her a while, trying to discern, maybe, whether it was a genuine offer.

'That'd be great,' she finally said. Mark would have said that meant she was giving Jacky the benefit of the doubt, accepting her niceties at face value. But Jacky saw the guardedness in people. Journalists were the worst of the lot, always looking for evidence of their own superiority. That was all this was. That was what human interaction was to people. Data for their self-justifying theories.

'Take a seat,' Jacky gestured to the long-line of the grey sofa in the far left of the room. Then turned to the espresso machine in the open-plan kitchen. She watched the journalist perch on the edge of the sofa, placing her satchel close to her feet. It pleased Jacky to see how the house encouraged compaction in people. It was as she intended. Their house was designed to be uncomfortable. It was designed so that people wouldn't stay too long. Guests would pass through in the way that Johnson, their architectural godfather, had stipulated, like fish. They should stay three days at most. To those who weren't at home in the vision, the degree of exposure would become unbearable. Jacky's skin was a cage to most.

She carried two perfect espressos to the journalist, who had already extracted a notepad. The cups clanged a little too loudly against the glass plate of their coffee table. The journalist peered down at the cup.

'Thanks. Do you have milk?'

The woman really was testing her.

'We're paleo.'

The journalist nodded and scribbled in her pad.

Jacky positioned herself on a chair across from the journalist, crossing her legs, sipping at the crema on her espresso, which always brought her comfort in times of stress.

'I have to admit, Jacky, you're not what I expected.'

'No?' Jacky heard the flat tone of the feigned interest she'd squeezed out of herself like an accordion.

'In that profile in *The Times*, if I'm honest, you came across as rather theatrical.'

'Yes, I was misrepresented.'

'I honestly found it refreshing. Starchitects with actual star qualities are few and far in between. It makes for some good reporting.'

'That's not really my concern.'

'Sure.'

A silence fell. Jacky could feel a swell of irritation taking hold of her. The usual frustration with an inept audience.

'I suppose what I'm asking is…You seem to have a strong perspective. Your work, how you present yourself, it's all connected by a palpable vision. I've interviewed quite a few architects and I haven't seen anything like it, the commitment you seem to have to design-living. And I'm wondering, where does that dedication come from? What gives you the confidence to live your design ethos?'

It was typical, this misinterpretation. Always misdirecting

the causal arrow, putting humans at the centre of that which they can't control.

'The way I present myself is a natural consequence of my design ethos. People forget that style is a product of a vision. It is not some static monument but a working argument. I don't take on my building's style, my buildings and my dress are a style that emerge from a way of seeing the world.'

Jacky sighed. She was slightly more relaxed now that she'd made her point. She looked at the journalist, who appeared to be listening, but, at this crucial moment, wasn't writing anything down. Perhaps she required further clarification.

'It isn't about me. It's about architecture.'

Jacky stared at the journalist, who nodded, but still wasn't taking notes. Instead, her head continued to bob irritatingly like a nodding dog.

'I must admit Jacky, I think that some would consider that a lofty justification for a clever marketing strategy. It might strike some people as disingenuous. Would it be too exposing to say that you're trying to make an impact?'

Jacky was starting to vibrate, the tethers of her muscles spasming the way they often did when she tried to explain herself to people.

'Buildings are aspirational. They represent an ideal. It's inaccurate to say I am trying to draw attention to myself. It misses the point.'

Jacky watched the journalist, still not writing. Her nervous system couldn't handle it. Her finger tips grew fuzzy, nerve endings searching for contact, firing into the void.

'I can give you an example if you like.'

'Please.'

'I had a disagreement with a client last week. I had to make a decision.'

Jacky paused, gathering her thoughts, but not too long, conscious that it could be misconstrued as theatrical.

'It was a moral decision as far as I was concerned, although I know that most would call it political. The thing is, I could have made it political but I chose to stick to my morals.'

Jacky reprimanded herself silently for even using the word political. Mark had told her to steer clear of politics. It was essential, he said, to be explicit about their politics as a company, but he was adamant that she left that to him. She swiftly redirected, using the language she knew.

'They wanted me to design a university building. A private liberal arts university in a pretty barren dead spot on the outskirts of London. Students with money wouldn't feel safe going there to learn about Marx, if you see what I mean.'

The journalist raised an eyebrow. Jacky scowled reactively. She didn't speak to people much; she underestimated her own venom for the times. She quickly went on.

'Unless the building captured their imaginations. You see, even socialist students are willing to invest in the capitalist machine when it makes them look good. University degrees are the most disingenuous tokens of progressive politics I can think of.'

'Where did you go to university?' The journalist asked, pen hovering, of course, to write that irrelevance down. Jacky refused to indulge her.

'Architecturally –'

Now she did pause – theatrically – to emphasise her refusal to get personal.

'Architecturally, the challenge appealed to me. Designing a building that would be conducive to learning. But I was very clear that learning precludes comfort. You don't learn within the parameters of your comfort zone. It was exciting, thinking about a wide-open atrium, an agora at the bottom, then layers of classrooms circling that open centre. How all of this would be made of glass, transparency being so fundamental to all of my buildings, and here, too, as an ideal for this academic community to aspire to. Lecturers would be able to watch students as they moved between lectures, as they talked and studied alone. Students, in turn, could be inspired by observing their professors at work. Transparency inspires self-respect, with everything on display we are challenged, to take responsibility for all of ourselves, to integrate our personalities into something consistent and principled. That is how the space we occupy can improve us. In that way my buildings aren't about people, or at least, only in the most radical sense, in that they show us how collectively, we can transcend ourselves, when we surrender to the natural laws of space and time. Everything I do, everything I am, is in service to that ideal.'

The journalist's face relaxed somewhat, Jacky was sure, resembling something close to interested attention. Jacky had found her stride.

'The university's managerial board were willing to hand the vision over to me. But they had a few stipulations. First, they wanted space to cultivate. Touches of green. Environmentalism being an important Leftist signifier.'

Jacky was finding her way back. She had drawn the journalist into the space she wanted to show her, the space she was always trying to share with everyone. Her politics, now, could be discussed architecturally. The way they should be. Now, she couldn't be misconstrued.

'When you refer to environmentalism as a signifier, am I to understand that you view these criteria as institutional greenwashing? Do you see yourself as complicit in that when you pander to these criteria?'

Jacky sighed. How did Mark do this? It was just too exhausting.

'I don't think signifiers are disingenuous. I wouldn't be an architect if I did. As I said, I see structures as symbols, I think they point to ideals. I appreciate institutions stating their values clearly.' The journalist tried to respond but Jacky intercepted. 'They also wanted modern with a nod to the Ancients on which their educational model was built. This I could also understand, in some ways my whole aesthetic revolves around a Platonic ideal. But then there was something I couldn't get on board with.'

'Which was?' The journalist leaned in now. And again, Jacky couldn't resist a dramatic pause, only because the situation demanded it.

'They wanted the design to cater to women's bodily needs.'

Jacky looked at the host, admittedly, with some sense of glee in anticipating the response. Only the journalist's face remained blank.

'Fair enough.'

Jacky hated talking to people. It made her feel alone. She had underestimated, once again, the overlap in the Venn diagram of respective worldviews. Ridiculousness for her fell easily within acceptable bounds for most. But she was determined to hold up a mirror.

'The Dean had read an article somewhere. About how the temperatures in offices are adjusted to men's body temperatures. She wanted her university to be designed for the comfort of women. And in that vein, she also wanted a feature she had noted with great enthusiasm in a building at one of her business meetings in Japan. A lactation room.'

Jacky searched the journalist's face for some sign of shared indignation, but realised suddenly that she probably wouldn't have recognised it even if she did. People were indecipherable.

'Again, to emphasise, I do not believe in designing for comfort. A lactation room has become a strange legal requirement for public establishments since a so-called Equality Act introduced in 2010. I've never liked the concept. Very Brave New World. Visions of women lined up. Tits strapped to industrial sized breast-pumps. I don't know, it's absurd to me. The idea of cordoning off an area just for these women, ushering them into a backroom like cattle. That's not something I'd want.'

'Maybe some women would feel safer.' The journalist said with a disdain that Jacky knew well.

'It doesn't matter. Like I said, it's not about making people comfortable. It's about challenging them to be better.'

The journalist looked down at her pad, frowned, then dropped it in some kind of performance of despondency. *Who's the theatrical one now?* Jacky scoffed.

'So, what I hear you saying, is that the women who feel uncomfortable with public breastfeeding need to work on themselves.'

A silence, charged, that much Jacky was able to discern.

'No, what I'm saying is, we all need to work towards an ideal, symbolised by the designs of my buildings, in which we all take full, individual responsibility for our existence.'

'I mean, sure, in an emancipated world we could all roam free with our bits hanging out. But that's not the world we live in, is it?'

'And it won't ever be if we keep tiptoeing around, censoring our bodies, and our beliefs.'

The journalist raised her voice, rising into that inevitable crescendo of all Jacky's human interactions.

'Point is, it's not safe for everyone to do that in the world we live in right now. Come on Jacky, don't be naïve. You're placing the onus of responsibility on women for a world that exposes them disproportionately to danger.'

'My buildings are ideals. They are meant to show us the best we can be.'

Jacky heard herself, and how stroppy she sounded. She hated this woman for reducing her to a petulant child. This is what people did with idealism – they belittled it. They turned it into naiveté.

'But they live in the world. You've been talking about taking responsibility for yourself. Don't you need to take responsibility for your work too? For how it affects peoples' lives?'

'I didn't want a lactation room in my university. So, I told them that. I told them that I couldn't agree to their terms.'

The journalist sighed and picked up her pad. 'Then what happened?'

'They conceded. We're going ahead.'

The journalist stared at Jacky in silence. It made her look stupid.

'Look, I didn't mean to make this political. I expressly didn't want to. I'm an architect, not a politician.'

'And you don't think that comes with a certain degree of social responsibility?'

'I just don't pretend to hold that degree of influence. It's actually a very humble position. I bow to nature, to the world as it is. Women breastfeed. I refuse to hide that. It's an ideal. And it's true: women who can't hack public breast feeding might want to avoid my buildings. And if my buildings end up sorting the strong from the weak, that's not my hand forcing anything, but a natural law we all know well. And those laws are timeless, and that's what will make my buildings meaningful to societies to come, and they wouldn't be if I pandered to trends.'

The journalist was scribbling furiously now. Frowning, as ever, with that generic sense for injustice. Jacky watched her while she drafted an email to Mark in her head, instructing him to squash the interview. Then the journalist stopped. Her face relaxed, and she smiled, actually beamed, announcing the end of the outrage that a moment ago had been insurmountable. The sudden shift exposed her disdain for what Jacky knew it was. All just a performance of belonging, through that same old mechanism of rejection. Jacky blinked to dispel any remnants of the illusion of any similarity between them – of all her ideas, that was the only one she would admit was utopian.

VERSES ON ENTOMOLOGY

Rainbow leaf beetle
Chrysolina cerealis
5.5-10mm

What a rare delight, to be blessed with the flamboyant splendour of the Rainbow leaf beetle. The metallic bands of green, blue, and gold of its back part to reveal red webbing. With those fierce and fiery wings, it blazes in flight. But only when the occasion calls for it. For fear of scaring off the other beetles. Most of the time, it walks, unassumingly, just like everyone else. Hiding its dragon-like ferocity.

The problem with that kind of camouflaging, is that the beetle also hides its potential from itself. As it learns to contain itself, memories of flight leave its body. Over generations, the rainbow leaf beetle loses its capacity for flight altogether. This is the slow and brutal mechanism, by which genius exits our species.

The rainbow leaf beetle is an endangered species. It cannot survive in the concrete silos of human complacency. Although some dispute the evidence for its dwindling population. They would rather make themselves complicit in a beetle's downfall, than give her the space she needs. Would rather banish her, than face the world they have made.

A strange and warped reality, where beetle-women too, rise and fall on the basis of human whims.

7

Mark told her to wait it out. Advice that Jacky saw for what it was: abandonment and betrayal. 'Let me do my job,' he said, alluding to their former trust in each other's abilities. She asked him when he'd be coming back, so that they could talk about it properly. He told her it would be a while. He tried to assuage her with the promise of a gift. Like she was some infant who needed to be placated.

The parcel arrived the following morning. A rectangular box wrapped in brown paper that she carried quickly from the door to the cooking island to unwrap. Mark often sent her gifts after a fight, a strange habit that never landed well for her. They both knew that she was perfectly capable of getting what she wanted. It was an uncomfortable gesture, a glitch in their alignment, a misrepresentation of who they were. Honestly, it was disrespectful. Despite her inner broil, she unwrapped the parcel carefully: there was never any justification for the unruliness of ripping or tearing. Diverting from her streamline would only be another form of surrender. She peeled off the Sellotape strips and folded back the flaps of paper like a book, revealing the contents to her. A framed, glass case, containing a taxonomy of beetles. She scoffed, but she leaned closer in. The beetles were arranged in a way that was pleasing to the eye; symmetrical, in order of size, and by gradations of colour, ranging from matte black to iridescent green. This wave of forms and light reached a pinnacle at the top of the frame where a single black and yellow specimen had been pinned with wings outspread, as if leading the swarm in their collective flight. Jacky blinked, the movement evoking the flutter of a beetle's wing that passed through her. She was captivated.

Jacky had spent a lot of time thinking about natural selection. It was one of the most beautiful natural processes she knew. An elegant theory based on the principle of absence. Perhaps partly as a consequence of its name, the process was often misconstrued as one based on advantage. As some invisible, God-like hand choosing the species it deems superior to live on as a new generation, or, perhaps, as an individual member of a species, consciously using their exceptional ability to propagate themselves. But the fittest didn't survive as a result of any inherent superiority. If anything, they are the products of mistakes. Of freakish mutations in sequences of genes that produces variation in the population. Suddenly, somewhere, a beetle is born with an aerodynamic body-shape that allows it to soar more efficiently than the rest. Their advantage is relative. The mechanism of evolution relies on variety, not superiority.

The beetles reminded Jacky of all of that. Their splendiferous tapestry was a mirror showing her the strength in her personality's mutation. The way the first article had named her The Beetle, erasing the process of her evolution. But Jacky would take heed of the lesson wrapped up in the glistening multicoloured sand of the beetle swarms' collective skin. She would embrace the mistake of her own existence. Because that was her advantage.

She had to admit, it was the encouragement she needed. Not that Mark would have given her the gift with any of her insights in mind. He saw nothing beyond literal resemblance. But Jacky had been reminded of the power of translation. How shapes moved through space and time. And it made her want to work.

Work was Jacky's answer to doubt. It wasn't really work, but the principle of acceleration. When she pushed through, against all expectations, against her physical limitations, and took flight. When the designs materialised before her just for a fleeting moment, only to be displaced by more, better, as she grasped for them in time. In that infinitely seductive swoosh was the thing she was chasing: coherence. For a moment, she made sense. She'd done away with the inner work people lazily talked about. She'd taken herself out of the equation. All she had to do was move fast enough to let the work convince her and everyone else of her value.

She stood behind her drafting board, pencil in hand, the way she still liked to work against the norms of an increasingly digitised profession. She stood hovering with that familiar sense of anticipation. Only today, it made her dizzy.

She sat down on a low metal stool across the room from her blank sheet of paper. Brought to a standstill, by the self-same energy that used to animate her. This is what came of meddling with order. Mark had shaken her, pushed her in counterintuitive directions, exposed her to criticism and doubt. It was all disorder and chaos. And it was more. As much as she hated to admit it, it was also doubt. She wondered where he was. She'd start to wonder, despite herself, where he was, what he was doing. Who he was with. She wasn't jealous, she didn't have time for jealousy, but she had underestimated how powerfully absence taunts the mind. How it invites you to imagine the worst-case scenario. It made her want to work even harder. But her body refused to move, had turned stiff as the back of her wooden chair. She'd been reduced to a fixture in the room.

Jacky pushed breath through her panic-stricken windpipe. The wheeze filled the room, circling back to stifle her. She released the weight of her body deeper into the hard surface beneath her. She reminded herself of her own postmodernism. Her resolution to embrace the various iterations of her identity. She looked down to scan her body. Her skin shone like glass, glistening with drops of humidity. It made sense – the house was humid with the dew of spring. That same moisture seemed to have gathered in the wrinkled folds of her armpits and collected on the ledge of her clavicles like rain in a gutter. Her body grew hot like the house around her, holding damp like a terrarium. This was new to her. Her body refusing to be disciplined. So wet, swollen, and fecund. Prime conditions for childbearing.

Jacky thought about the beetles. She pictured them again: their order and relationships, their modular diversity. She wasn't blocked, she told herself, she was changing. Growth was painful, and so pain was necessary. She was growing a new beetle skin. Jacky pushed her back into her chair as shadows sliced through her cube of carefully constructed space. She sat there all day and into the night, resolutely still, absorbing darkness, sitting there in her human-sized vase, like an orchid dipped in dye.

8

'*My buildings will sort the strong from the weak*
– Jacky MacKenzie on the eugenics of architecture.'

Mark had read the article. Of course he had. It was everywhere. And it was shocking. He'd picked up a paper copy, thinking, stupidly, that it would be a nice bit of memorabilia for the archives. He re-read it while wheeling his shopping trolley down the cereal aisle of his favourite Swedish supermarket in Paddington. A place he turned to in difficult times. It sold all the treats he'd discovered over the course of his many business trips to Stockholm – some lean, light and sufficiently bland not to incite too much guilt (he was still paleo in spirit). Things like crispbread and caviar and milky-coloured cheeses, or like the strong black coffee that punched you in the face when you so much as opened the pack. But then there was the really exciting part – the laser show of highly artificial sweets. All the shapes. Lurid red fish and neon green snakes, sticky streaks of liquorice, strings of sour spaghetti. He'd developed a real sweet tooth in recent years. Perhaps it was the calorie deficit of their restricted diet, or just the lack of stimulation that came of sugarless subsistence. One thing he knew: they came in handy in times like these.

His London flat had become a veritable bachelor pad. White powder strewn across the gleaming surfaces, an onlooker could have mistaken the sugar crush for a coke addiction. Sometimes he considered making the transition, but he'd seen what it did to the business tycoons he worked with, how they descended into chattering, self-indulgence, self-loathing. He imagined what Jacky would think of him: 'loser', she'd say. That would be worse than anything. She had no respect for him. She already walked all over him, controlled everything he did. She'd crept in with her streamlining and she wouldn't let go. She was there even when she wasn't. Guiding his hand to the healthy products, criticising him for every snuff of sugar that touched his lips. She wouldn't release her grip, even for a second. And he let her. She called out and he answered. He enabled her sonar vision. That's why he'd told her his double life, this exhausting, parallel half-existence, was further away than it was; she wouldn't send her soundwaves to Sweden, and so he couldn't answer them. Look what she'd reduced him to. He tipped another scoop of confectionary into shiny plastic and dumped it in his trolley.

This was him attending to his own needs because no one else would. Had Jacky thought of him, when she decided to discount every piece of advice he'd given her and air her bigotry with the world? Had she thought about the hard work he'd done when she ruined this latest interview by being so pathologically unlikable? Or what about the way she'd worn him down, with years of unacknowledged labour. All the mopping up, all the relationship management he'd been doing ever since they met. Behaving like her vision justified it all. The vision he had to make people care about. The vision that would otherwise have remained what it was when he found it. Just an intellectualised form of severe OCD.

He needed sugar today. He noted the fluctuations of his anger, trying to breathe through them the way he'd read in a self-help book he kept at his apartment. Self-help books were definitely *not* streamlined. Jacky would kick him in the nuts if she saw him with it.

Metaphorically, of course, although he did worry. She was so unhinged these days. She'd always been eccentric but when they started building their house, something snapped. She used to be so restrained; that had always been one of her redeeming features. There was something appropriately apologetic about it. Despite her lack of people skills, it made you feel like she didn't mean to offend anyone. It was impressive, there was something superhuman in how she managed to contain her personality. He'd respected her for it.

Mark breathed and tuned into his physical sensations, the way the book had taught him to. He noticed heat creeping up his neck. He knew it was going red. He hated how that looked. That inflamed fleshiness bulging over the white of his shirt collar. He always felt restricted by suits. His body was too long for them, so they looked too tight, too short, and his feet poked out disproportionately. In the mornings, when he looked in the mirror, his appearance would annoy him. He looked like a T-square.

But he didn't let that get in the way. People respected him all the same. He'd worked hard for that. The familiar sweat patches now spread under his armpits, fuelled by his circular rage, gathering in a cloud of sour body odour. He hated that smell. He prided himself on personal hygiene. It made him even angrier. Now his tummy hurt. He needed to relax.

He unboxed his earbuds to tune into some Swedish techno. He slipped the curvaceous pods into his earholes, hunching his long frame over the trolley, as he pushed on, eyes darting between the smorgasbord to his right and the newspaper still perched on the handlebar in front of him.

He'd told her to stay away from politics. She did this stuff to torment him, he knew it, to pull him back in. These were her tactics. All her talk about space and independence. Truth was, she didn't know how to handle herself. She barely knew when she was hungry, let alone how she actually felt. She was always on the edge of collapse and he'd been molly-coddling her for years. With words of encouragement, little gestures, whatever she needed to keep going. He'd stooped to new depths with the latest attempt at an ego boost. *Beetles for The Beetle.* He knew she'd drink it up. She didn't have the emotional toolkit to get through life, let alone a relationship, and he was exhausted. He threw something sweet and sticky in his mouth and leaned in to inspect the shadowy picture that accompanied the article. He zoomed in on Jacky, how she sat curled over on the edge of her seat like a scared insect. And he wasn't sure if he wanted to pick her up and hold her in his hand, or sever her little body with an extra salty liquorice stick.

9

In between Mark's absences and his presences, and throughout all the ups and downs of Jacky's life, there was Clarissa. She called Clarissa when he was gone. Clarissa always told her to pack it up and move in with her. But Jacky couldn't, because if Clarissa loved her the way she was in those moments, she reasoned, then she didn't love her for who she really was. Jacky would tell Clarissa that and then Clarissa would tell her to get real. 'Get real,' in her Canadian drawl, and for a moment, Jacky would let Clarissa be her reality.

Jacky started seeing Clarissa in the early days, when she and Mark were still fresh, and when she was still adjusting to the patches of solitude they'd designed into their relationship. Then, later, she'd see her during Mark's longer stints in Stockholm, where, she was by then pretty sure, he had someone else, beautiful, conventionally feminine, who propped him up the way Clarissa did her.

She'd visit her in Brighton. Clarissa would buy fish and chips at a crumbling place near the pier and tell her to 'eat up.' And she would. Then they'd go back to her damp, dim terraced one-bedroom and drink red wine on her old yellow second-hand sofa, nestling further into the human-sized dents in its cushions with every glass. They'd be asleep by midnight and the next day Clarissa would spoon her most of the morning, carrying her through the melodrama of a red wine hangover. It would pass by mid-afternoon. Then they'd stroll in the sea air, watching the cloudy grey sky turn to black. In the evening they'd cook. Spaghetti Bolognese. Sometimes a meaty oven dish. Warmth and flesh Jacky didn't get from her bento boxes of raw vegetables. That's what Clarissa gave Jacky – permission. Jacky never really understood what she gave Clarissa in return.

'You make me laugh,' she'd tell her when she asked. 'At you, of course.'

Jacky wasn't sure if she liked how Clarissa humoured her. It wasn't what she was used to. With Mark, that would have been antithetical to love.

'No silly, I laugh at you because I love you. Laughter is light and love is about lighting up the dark before we die.'

Clarissa would say things like that, and Jacky would forget for a moment how competent Clarissa was. How she could fix up boats, minds, and the bodies of humans. The boats were more like patients to her and the patients more like teachers. She'd say things like that, and it would make Jacky love her more although she didn't understand what she meant. Coming from Clarissa, combinations of words made sense less literally. It was only later, when she looked back on their time together from between the crisp white sheets of her own home, that it all seemed put on, falsely modest, overly sentimental.

Jacky called Clarissa the night after the interview. Then repeatedly over the week that followed, as the journalist continued to ping her messages, asking about her personal life. She called her mainly at night, when the transparent glass turned impenetrable black.

'She's just fishing, don't answer,' Clarissa kept saying. She didn't understand, of course, that they'd fill the void of her silence with misinterpretations.

'I thought you said you were OK with that?'

Clarissa was right. Jacky's resolve to embrace her multiplicity had dwindled. Something about the convolution had made her crabby and eager for a fight.

The media loved it of course. Maybe word had gotten out that she was a fun ride. After the first interview was released, they kept calling her for interviews and she agreed to them. She had to channel her raging motion somewhere, now that she couldn't work.

'Listen to this. "She calls it *streamlining*, evoking the aerodynamic shapes of her designs. One of the many ways in which MacKenzie aims to pass her cut-throat philosophy as a design ethic – a move we might recognise in the aestheticized philosophies of most dictatorships."'

Clarissa didn't respond. That always unnerved Jacky, who was never sure whether to interpret the silence as attentive or disinterested. In that way, Clarissa was still unfamiliar to her.

'Isn't it ridiculous?'

Clarissa hmm-ed on the other end of the line.

'I spent an hour talking to this woman and this is what she came up with. She arrived with her mind made up. People don't listen.'

Jacky waited for Clarissa's usual cooing affirmation. But she said nothing.

'A bit of support would be appreciated right now.'

A sigh. Clarissa cleared her throat.

'I struggle sometimes because we talk things through, and we come to new insights, and then it seems to go poof.'

'This is entirely out of my control.'

'But we talked about what this decision would mean, taking a more public role, remember? We talked about how it would bring some challenges. How you'd have to let go. That you can't control what people think.'

Jacky vaguely remembered the conversation, how it had helped reconcile her with the decision to go ahead with the interview. How it had left her feeling strengthened and prepared. But Clarissa didn't fully appreciate the schism between their respective realities. Emotions were Clarissa's job, while, for Jacky, they were a discordant undertone distracting her from work. She didn't have time for emotions. In the blazing state of emergency of her every day they weren't a priority.

'Why don't you come to Brighton for the weekend? Rest up.'

'I have a deadline.'

'It might be our last chance for a while.'

'Are you finally sailing away?'

'I have a feeling you are.'

Jacky groaned. 'Don't be so dramatic.'

The silence lingered, alive with possible endings. Jacky was always tempted to cut things off with Clarissa. The whiff of a complication was enough to trigger a threat. Clarissa told her it was emotionally manipulative. But it was a natural response – Clarissa posed a major threat to the streamline.

'Mark will think it's a good thing. No press is bad press, right?' Jacky winced at her own pathetic pleading.

Clarissa scoffed. 'For him maybe.'

Jacky ignored the comment. Clarissa seemed to resent Mark. She was so determined to demonise him. Petty behaviour for a therapist.

'Where is Mark?'

Jacky turned to the wall of glass to her left, taking in the reflection of her face, clearer than the rest of her body in the light of her phone screen angled against her ear. It was blue, gaunt, barely human. She hadn't heard from Mark since the article. It wasn't entirely unexpected. He was probably embarrassed. His master plan had backfired. This is what happened when he tried to take control of the partnership. He needed time to humble himself and come around. But it was taking longer than expected.

'Just remember you have options. This could be a new start for you. You could come here. Do something totally different. Get away from the noise. It doesn't have to eat away at you.'

'Who says it is?' Jacky snapped. She breathed deeply, heat rising in her claustrophobic lungs. Clarissa was always doing this, telling her she had 'options', making her out to be some kind of shipwreck, as if her career success didn't make any anxiety she might feel worthwhile.

'I wish you'd just listen when I called. Not try to fix things.' Jacky heard herself become child-like when she talked to Clarissa. She regressed. It was easy. She enjoyed and resented it.

'You know that's my thing.'

A Scarab Where the Heart Should Be

'Your thing is getting boring.' Jacky hung up and stood pouting, hyperaware of the invisible walls around her. She felt trapped, and unutterably bored, as she stood still as a pillar, spiralling into the night.

VERSES ON ENTOMOLOGY

Rose Chafer
Cetonia aurata
20mm

The Rose Chafer is recognised most obviously by its metallic shine. In emerald green and shades of purple-bronze, it glistens like an oil slick in the sun. You will find her among the leaves and petals of grasslands, scrubs and woodland edges. You must look carefully to spot the camouflaged studs. With their subtle shades of depth, they reveal a nuance that is different from the surrounding fronds of even colour. But to appreciate them in all their splendour, you will have to reconsider what you thought you knew.

How does the Rose Chafer acquire its iridescent shine? Iridescence is the product of microscopic structures that are fine enough to interfere with visible light. Unlike pigments, that absorb light, these patterns work like prisms to bend and refract. Iridescence is less colour than a differential geometry.

Iridescence is a beautiful shield. Part camouflage, part armour, it is an effortless defence. Armed with invisible structures, the rose chafer survives the brightness of the sun's penetrating light. For a woman like Jacky, there was much to learn from this ability to hide behind a distracting sheen. She had always stood out, her outstanding abilities set her apart, and distracted people from her inner complexity. She knew the physics of these refractions intimately. It was her default mode of being. And yet, it was validating, to find that her tactics mirrored by the natural world. It made her feel less alone. Connected not just to the rose chafer, but to all the beetles with their individual survival mechanisms. Bound by a universal need, differentiated by their respective approaches. She had chosen to shine like a rose chafer. Others hid in dung. But all of them had chosen. Hers was just one of the beetle's many skins.

10

The critics hadn't always been so critical. Nor so ubiquitous. Jacky remembered, that Sunday, as she hunched over her laptop, taking in the malignant growth of coverage across the internet, their earliest reviews. How they'd been clean and clear, and unclouded by the smog of judgement. They'd called the buildings Scandinavian at first. In the beginning, they'd generously overlooked her 'modernist tendencies', so male-centric in their lack of concern with domestic life. They'd given her the benefit of the doubt. Her style, they said, prioritised simplicity and connectedness, and, by implication, activities like cooking, cleaning, tending to gardens. That's how they'd landed on a traditionally feminine interpretation of her ambitious minimalism. Jacky was promoting domesticity, they wrote, a return to the female, a rejection of manmade structures and a manmade world. Her houses were reviewed in the magazines reserved for the world's *crème de la crème* of architects, but appreciated for the *crème* more than the cachet. Until they decided they weren't considered good for either.

In the recent onslaught of articles, however, they saw ruthlessness everywhere. In her abrasive, clipped speech, her unfriendly buildings. No one ever laughed at her jokes but she maintained a flippant attitude towards her interviewers, they wrote. She didn't seem to notice their distaste, or, once again, didn't care. They saw it, too, in her relationship, her partner's telling absence. They quoted her comment about her streamlined ovaries. They especially went on about her ovaries.

There was also the inevitable speculation about her 'leaning in'. Maybe she adopted an air of hostility, the more lenient journalists wrote, to compete in architecture's boy club. Although that didn't seem to redeem her. In one article, they charted the progression of Jacky's appearance over the years, how her body had become ever-trimmer, and her face ever-meaner, in direct proportion to her growing success. One cartoonist charted the transformation as a parody of an ape's evolution into a human, showing Jacky morphing from an attractive looking woman, into a mannish-looking bug. The argument the journalists were making, Jacky deduced, was that it was becoming impossible to ignore the patterns of her personality. And yet, they couldn't see the beauty in that.

She would have accepted the character assassination if they'd got the architecture right. The Beetle was supposed to help them understand. But their early misinterpretations of her style had brought them closer to the truth – in so far as it brought them closer to the architecture. In the early days, with that misnomer of Nordic progressive living, they saw the work, at least. They commented on the designs. They'd even celebrated her corporate projects – those sharp and angular skyscrapers. They jutted out of the ground like blades of grass, they said. Now, those blades of grass had turned to phalluses (evidence of her unbridled megalomania, naturally). Quite a leap, you'd think, not just in meaning but in function too. It made her anxious, to imagine the world through their eyes, of objects shapeshifting like that.

She tried to call Mark but he didn't answer. Fearing the ossifying effect of her drawing board, she turned instead to new entomological investigations. She'd been inspired by Mark's gift, she had to admit. She'd ordered a set of drawers, forceps and pins, determined to start a larger collection. She knew the importance of arming yourself with the right tools – both manual and conceptual. She was educating herself on the splendiferous range of designs out there. The magnitude of the beetle's natural variation. She'd set up the drawers in her work room, alongside her drawing board, in the hope that their proximity would invite a conceptual synergy, and inspire new work. In that sense, she wasn't wasting time at all on this new, and probably first ever, hobby. It was all part of the same picture.

But one obstacle had presented itself to her. In order to build her collection, she'd have to go outside. And as much as she could appreciate the godly architecture of the great outdoors from afar, she wasn't in the mood to enter into it. The thought of it, in fact, struck her as mildly terrifying. She narrowed her pupils to focus on the glass of the walls rather than looking through them. Her distance from nature had been made stronger by the transparency of the walls. She took that distance for granted. It had made her arrogant. Weathering storms untouched, she'd started to feel invincible. But just the thought of her foot sinking into the slippery mud sent electric dread down her spine. She wrapped her arms around her cold and brittle shoulders, conscious of her eggshell constitution. She heard a sudden shrieking – maybe a fox? Maybe mortality's warning cry.

Where was Mark?

She needed a body, a strong and steady buttress. She needed him not because she was weak, but because humans depended on the structures they built to protect themselves.

She'd had a discussion with Clarissa about it once. The one and only time that she'd tried to let Clarissa into her conceptual world. She'd taken her to a public lecture on architecture. It was back in the early days, when she hadn't consolidated the necessary configuration of her relationships, which came to depend on conceptual and physical separation. She'd deluded herself into thinking that Clarissa could be a part of her world with Mark.

'What makes us human?' the professor had asked in that grandiose style they favoured when talking to a general audience. Jacky didn't mind. It was important to impress on people that architecture is deeply existential.

There was the predictable silence that Jacky recalled from her university lectures. It still made her just as impatient. She'd quickly raised her hand.

'That we can innovate, and hereby domesticate our environment.'

The professor beamed at having discovered a student so adept.

'That's exactly right. The defining aspect of modern humanity has been their drive to domesticate nature. Most people refer to the agricultural revolution as the pivotal phase, but it started earlier than that, with the discovery of fire, which in turn led to cooking, which caused our brains to evolve. And so evolution has depended on a process that has been as much artificial as natural. We manufactured our own evolution, as our bodies and minds changed through the interaction of tools and environment. In that sense and that sense alone, it is fair to say, that human beings are close to the Divine.'

Jacky had revelled in the familiar origin story; every architect had their own translation, but the underlying sentiment was always the same: architecture was life. She remembered then, looking to Clarissa, hoping to share her enthusiasm, as she was accustomed to, with the person she loved. But Clarissa wouldn't look at her. Her, even back then, weather-torn face looked straight ahead.

The lecture went on.

'The domestication of wheat was instrumental to the agricultural revolution. People turned from hunting and gathering, to farming. They cultivated forms of wheat with spikes that didn't shatter when they dispersed their seeds like their wild predecessors. This allowed farmers to harvest wheat to meet demand. Populations grew. That was the beginning of society as we know it.'

That was when Clarissa chose to speak.

'It was also the beginning of patriarchy as we know it, but I'm sure that's not what we're going to talk about.'

Jacky flinched. It was the first cruel thing she'd ever heard Clarissa say.

'That's what you're thinking? We've just heard this brilliant, deeply human insight, that we aren't slaves to our environment. That we can manipulate it. That we have this degree of agency that sets humans apart from the rest of the animal kingdom. That we have this unique opportunity to make something meaningful.'

'Alright, here's my story. Society stormed in and made its demands on vegetation, and it seemed that the plants obeyed. Only it wasn't about us. We'd misunderstood. Ignored the evidence that there were forces bigger than us. That transcended us. That knew how to live despite us, not for us, and that outlive us after we've gorged ourselves and died. That story about us bending nature to our will is old and wrong. The story of wheat is about how we destroyed that plant's ability to disperse its seeds. We've colonised it. We've made it dependent on us. In a sense we've killed it. All because we need to convince ourselves that our lives are meaningful. And not just that, we've claimed vast areas of land that no longer have the biodiversity it needs to keep the climate in balance, and so our clever humanity, in the end, will kill us too. This is the kind of thinking that kills us all, Jacky, and it makes me sad that you believe any of it.'

They walked home in silence. Jacky was disturbed by the conversation. Clarissa had disagreed with her in a way Mark never had. Clarissa had told her that her thinking was structurally flawed. And, although she needed to dismiss it all, to protect the foundations of her design ethos, it didn't make her want to push Clarissa away. In fact, it made her want to have sex with her. So they did, the second they got home. Things with Clarissa were like that – they made no conceptual sense, didn't need to. She was an incontestable truth. A buttress like no other. A strong and steady counterforce. Jacky never took Clarissa to another work-related event again, but not because she feared her views, only because that single experience had explained everything.

It rained that night that Jacky decided not to go beetle hunting. For the first time since she'd moved into the house, water turned her clear glass into a murky plastic sheath. She looked up at the droplets, how they grew bulbous, then burst into smaller parts. She imagined letting the rain wash over her. She spread herself across the kitchen floor, limbs extended like the tendrils of a creeper. She opened her mouth wide, waiting for the droplets to make their way, somehow, against the odds, through the forcefield of glass, to her dry and thirsty tongue. In a different configuration, with Clarissa by her side, perhaps she would find a way, to let them in and through. In that moment, it seemed like the most natural thing in the world, to go and see her.

11

Jacky always liked the image of herself in the black, bug-eyed tin of her Volkswagen Beetle hurtling down the country lanes. She liked to imagine herself in bird's eye, her movements both trivial and inevitable. Usually dishevelled, skin murky like she'd been dipped in caffeine, she'd get in that car, pull the sun visor down and apply a lipstick in bright red. Another metamorphosis.

Her lips were her mating call. That red was the only colour she let into her monochrome existence. She only ever wore lipstick for Clarissa. She was the only person Jacky wanted to be attractive to. She wanted Mark's respect. But she wanted Clarissa to melt at the sight of her.

She called Clarissa on hands-free as she drove, feeling distinctly whimsical, gazing out over the dabbled hedgerows, sunlight on her face.

'I'm coming to see you.'

'You're schizophrenic.'

'You're the therapist, but surely that diagnosis is a bit of a stretch.'

'It's not a diagnosis, it's a prognosis.'

Jacky scoffed, then her throat constricted in a way that

was becoming increasingly common.

'I need to see you.'

'You only ever visit when you do.'

Jacky indicated left, then turned onto wide tarmac, pressing her snub-nosed shoe hard on the accelerator.

'It's not that I don't love you.'

'I know, you've just never learnt how to express it.'

Clarissa was always trying to get Jacky to talk about her childhood. As if all the answers to their misaligned aspirations lay complete and whole, buried in the past. Jacky refused to do what Clarissa called 'inner child work.' But she repeatedly reassured her that there were no answers to be found there. There was a null where her childhood memories should have been. That was how she could best describe it, and she had tried to find the words, grasping for an answer that could satisfy people. Null was the best she could come up with. An infinite loop connoting emptiness. Her childhood had taken place in that zero of a void. She had been birthed by parents who were voids. Both of them pale and downtrodden emblems of the British middle class who themselves were the products of a lineage of infinite regressing voidness. Those were the microstructures that had shaped the conditions for her later life: boring, dead and passionless. Her parents, when she brought them to mind, were generic and incredibly far away. Like the pictures in a book teaching children vocabulary. Under their picture was the word, 'parents', in block letters – bold, reductive, containing an imperative –this was a word you *had* to learn, regardless of what it meant to you. She could barely remember their faces. She didn't speak to them beyond perfunctory phone-calls of congratulations when they came across her buildings in their Sunday paper or a travel magazine. It had always been that way. They weren't parents who talked, or loved, or expressed anything.

It wasn't just Clarissa, of course. People were always asking her about childhood. The reporters liked to ask her, to confirm their suspicions about her beetle character. As if childhood memories were a prerequisite for a heart. Jacky had tried to tell them that the privileging of childhood as a marker of empathy was a form of elitism. But she soon realised she wasn't going to convince anyone. Usually she made something up.

'I need you, you know.'

Clarissa laughed at that, with her usual performed levity, which Jacky gratefully took at face value. Both pretending that nothing Jacky did hurt her.

'Behind every great woman is another great woman. The question is, why we gotta be so great?'

They talked on hands-free until Jacky arrived at her door. Clarissa opened it, that door painted red, like Jacky's lips. She opened it and they kissed and they tumbled into her narrow hall, where Jacky pushed her against the wall and ran her hands through her soft grey curls, then along the strong square of her shoulders, grabbing for the seam of her shirt in those nautical stripes she lived in. Jacky rolled the stretch cotton up and over her head and kissed her stomach, leaving a trail of red lipstick like footsteps from the spot between her breasts down to her bellybutton. She traced the line with her index finger, smudging the steps into a stream.

Jacky always worried, for a moment after the passion of reunion settled, that their affection was spent. But their love only seemed to unfold, each layer deeper, stronger, more integral. They lay silently on the floor of the narrow hall, Clarissa's naked body pressed against hers, and hers pressed against the wall.

'I bought a boat,' Clarissa eventually said.

'Finally.' Jacky pressed her ear against Clarissa's neck and listened to the warm hum of her laughter.

'I guess it was about time. Can't spend my life fixing other people's boats.' She poked Jacky in her side. Jacky rolled her eyes.

'I bought it off this Vet. Old white dude. Alcoholic, of course. I offered him the full amount upfront. When he heard my accent, he yelled at me to take the bloody boat, sail it all the way home and teach those yanks a thing or two about loyalty.'

'You tried to reason with him, didn't you?'

Clarissa smiled. 'I just thought it might make it easier for him to find closure knowing his baby was going to a Canadian.'

'People are unreasonable. I wish you'd just accept that.'

'Life is unreasonable. People are just trying to make sense of it. And we end up looking in some weird-ass places.'

'People don't want to change their minds.'

She tilted her head, eyebrows raised. 'I know.'

Jacky looked into her lover's pebble-coloured eyes. 'Not now.'

'You're limiting yourself.' There she was again, with her strong stance, her unrelenting opinion that made Jacky want to push and pull.

'If you're talking about us moving in together, I can't.'

'I've come so far. I have to see it through. There's a time to anchor and a time to sail, right?'

'You're not happy. You keep coming here, and calling, because you're not happy.'

Jacky shifted fractionally away from her, back pressing against the radiator on the wall, suddenly scorching, making her itchy and hot. She looked at her lover, feeling wispy thin across from her solid certainty.

'I couldn't do the work without Mark. And he wouldn't have the humility to collaborate if I was living with you.'

'He's holding you hostage.'

'It's not... I want it too.'

That was hard for Jacky to say to Clarissa.

'Where is he now Jacky?'

'It's just a fight.'

'But where is he every time you're in trouble?'

'It doesn't matter. That's not what it's about. We're building something. That's uncomfortable sometimes.'

'You've built a mutually enabling structure. You're stuck in a tautology that doesn't make sense.'

That was the closest Clarissa had ever come to speaking her language. It was like she was growing ruthless too, determined to convince her by any means. Or maybe they'd just known each other longer than she realised. They were all meant to exist as separate walls, connected by space. But maybe it was only inevitable that, after a while, you started to merge. Despite her best efforts, perhaps they'd started that process of two becoming one. Maybe that force towards convergence, however unnatural it had always seemed to her, was a natural inclination.

Jacky sighed. 'Why are you always pushing me to change?'

Clarissa stared at her, almost through her. As she did, her

expression darkened, a cloud passing across the ripples of her face. She looked tired and wise.

'A child went missing here last week. It happens so much. People just lose them to the sea.'

Jacky stared at her. Clarissa often told stories about people Jacky didn't know. It wasn't that they were uninteresting, just that she always told them in moments that made them seem irrelevant. They weren't part of the story that connected them, and so they didn't make much sense to her.

'How did you hear about it?' She tried.

Clarissa easily saw through Jacky's inauthenticity. But she was never put off. She always called Jacky a 'slow burner', said it just took her a while to care, because she was so distracted, not because she was cold. She was the only person ever to have insisted on Jacky's heart like that.

'The mum is a regular client. Been seeing her every week for years. That week she showed up with a broken ankle. She'd slipped in the shallows after she'd run into the water looking for him. She refused to go to the doctor, so her husband had made her come to talk to me.'

Jacky tried to exercise her imagination. She really did try for Clarissa. To conjure an image of the woman flailing in knee-deep water. But it only seemed mildly ridiculous.

'She kept saying "I wanted it to be a perfect day".'

'That's very sad.' Jacky offered, sensing, at the very least, that that would be appropriate to say.

'No, it's more than that. I know she wasn't negligent, but her saying how she wanted it to be perfect, it just made me think. I kept imagining their day, like one of those romantic flashbacks in a film. Like the mum, pristine, perfect, in a floral dress, packing the picnic, obsessing over details. A perfect little picnic, perfect outfits for the children, perfectly packed car, perfectly planned route. And, I know it wasn't their fault, of course not, that's really not what I'm saying, but it just made me think how we ruin things by trying to make them so perfect. I always tell my clients, you know, focus on what you can control, not what you can't. People spend their lives obsessing over what they can't control. And they miss it all, they miss what's going on out there, like the ocean, they forget to look at it because they're scared. But that's exactly when it'll get you.'

Jacky waited the appropriate length of time not to sound dismissive.

'You're just trying to find agency where there is none. Shit happens.'

'For fuck's sake Jacky, you're so goddamn literal. I'm trying to tell you something.'

Jacky looked away, feeling unnervingly inept. This is what happened when she stopped. A familiar blankness that had trailed her since childhood. Blankness like a big zero, frayed around the edges, blurring into threads of subtle panic that became the fabric of her existence. No one should have to surrender to that kind of paralysing fear. No one deserved to live like that. It was her right to run. Acceleration was a human dignity.

Clarissa spared Jacky the embarrassment, or the pain, of asking her what she meant. She softened and wrapped her arms around her.

'Just try to break out of your tunnel vision every once in a while.'

A Scarab Where the Heart Should Be

Jacky didn't know what that meant either, she felt the panic move from the fibres of her muscles to her head, facial muscles contracting uncontrollably, mouth opening into a hollow 'O'. She leaned into Clarissa, who rocked her, not asking, never asking her to explain her fear away.

12

In some ways, Jacky's childhood *had* been formative. In that it had given her the most fundamental lesson in form. That zero of time and space had showed her that you can create something out of nothing simply by drawing a line around it. Creating wasn't conjuring – it was restricting. Everything already existed. Architects weren't gods, and despite what people seemed to think, Jacky did know that. Architects only changed people's perceptions of the spaces they inhabited. They were illusionists. They weren't utopian, they just tried to put an idea to work, to make it stand. They weren't cynics either because they had ideals. But they didn't delude themselves in thinking that their ideas would be more or less than the structure that held them. That made architects brave. They accepted their limitations and put them on display. They made the best of the mind, the hands, and the tools available to them, and then they made themselves accountable for bodies and lives. They took a form of responsibility that other artists didn't, and that most people didn't. They made themselves accountable, in a very real sense, for their own coherence, no matter how unromantic that picture might be.

Jacky had to remind herself, why she was proud to be an architect that day.

'The new you is making waves. Maybe you're onto something.'

'What d'you mean? People hate me.'

Mark had finally recovered from his tantrum and made an appearance. Jacky knew he would, that he'd be unnerved by the silence that tended to accompany her happiness. He couldn't bear not being needed. She pictured Clarissa raising her eyebrow knowingly at her from her boat on a sunny sea.

'Don't play dumb, you're milking it. But maybe that's a good thing. Maybe I was wrong about trying to behave. This is your style.'

'What? Fascist?'

'Ruthless.'

They were drinking espressos on the sofa, the one they had chosen with their cohabitation in mind. Jacky remembered the last time they'd sat there. By now, it was maybe a month ago. How they'd had breakfast there the morning they moved in. Warm cinnamon buns and fresh espresso. A respectful nod to their respective affiliations; a collaborative communion.

'You're making me out to be some kind of strategic mastermind. I'm just doing what you told me. And it's gone down as I said it would. This is not how we work.'

He rolled his eyes and Jacky closed hers. She let the morning sun warm her ghostly skin, relax the muscles in her forehead that had been pulled into a knot by the flood of beings nibbling at her. She inhaled the smooth bitterness of her espresso. Just espresso today.

'Social justice warriors always shoot themselves in the foot. It'll sort itself out.'

Mark stared at her, haughty, pouting. If Jacky was honest with herself, she'd have to admit that this version of Mark, this generic PR robot, hadn't appeared suddenly. He'd been perfectly consistent; populist, you could say, or pragmatic, adopting the rhetoric he needed to advance his interests. He'd chosen the language he needed to convince her. Now he was speaking in a new winy cadence – the voice of marketized politics, of social justice slogans, of 'social currency' and 'brand identity'. Jacky hadn't changed either. She'd always been out of step with the world. And so maybe their divergence had been inevitable. Mark had always been bound to be swept along by the fickle tides of influence and she'd always been bound to stick to her course.

'It's how the whole pro-life movement started. Don't you know the story? How no one took notice of the evangelists until the feminists started protesting outside their churches. Then the whole religious community rallied against them. Give feminists an enemy, and they'll propel them to fame. That's what they do.'

He scoffed. 'What podcast have you been listening to?'

'It's true.'

'So that's what you want, then? Fame. More attention.' He smirked and Jacky wanted to slap him.

'I just want to be left to do my work how I want to do it. Which is why I agreed to this partnership.'

The eye roll made a reappearance. The eye roll that was supposed to tell her how exhausting she was. It made him look like a teenager.

'I'm tired, you know.'

His eyeball darted back, caught truanting.

'It's not easy, being the bloody dung beetle.'

He scoffed. With contempt.

'I'm serious. I'm the one out there.'

'Yes. You're the one out there making a spectacle of yourself. Making frankly insane decisions. How the hell did you turn an interview about architecture into a fascist manifesto? You think you're tired? We're the ones always cleaning up the shit.'

His deviant eyeballs now darted in all directions, evading responsibility for the dangerous pronoun he'd let slip.

We. Jacky narrowed her eyes at him, daring him to drag Clarissa across the boundaries they'd solemnly drawn. He met her gaze for a while, deciding, probably, how low he was prepared to stoop. Eventually he backed down, like he always did. He brought his empty espresso cup to his mouth and pretended to take a sip.

'You chose to be the front man, Jacky. Can we finally be honest about that?'

'Not like this.'

'You should've seen it coming. You hurt people's feelings. This is what happens. You always think you're exempt from social rules.'

Mark sighed, got up and stretched his long body.

'Anyway, it doesn't matter. Like I said, I think we should lean into it.'

Lean into it. More of that coded language Jacky couldn't stand. How it personified businesses, like they had interests and feelings. Implying that whatever grotesque strategy he was proposing was as innocuous as a person's penchant to be liked.

'You need to get on Twitter.'

She looked at him, for the first time, totally out-of-love.

'Can we please agree to maintain some level of integrity.'

'I'm telling you. This is important. All the big firms are doing this kind of thing now.'

'You do it then.'

He tilted his head like a sarcastic teenager. 'You know it needs to come from you.' He smirked, couldn't resist: 'You're *The Beetle*.'

There it was again, that new, confusing dissection of what they were.

'You might like it. It's an opportunity you've never had. The space to explain yourself, without people's reactions throwing you off. It might be your platform.'

'My platform is architecture.'

'Do it, Jacky. We need to ride this wave or it could drown us.'

Jacky thought again of Clarissa on her boat, and, for some reason, of the disappearing child. Of his little body floating face down in the sea. A shudder ran through her.

'I need to get going.' He wanted to avoid the night, of course, with its complicated invitation of intimacy. 'We'll Zoom in the morning if you need help getting started.'

'Where are you going?'

He frowned at her, reproachful. That was a question they never asked. That rule, conveniently, still stood for him.

Jacky stood up and scurried to the glass wall, staring after him as he left, blinking in the glare of the car lights. She stood there, feeling small and pinched and, at the same time, heavy under the weight of her long, black blazer, trailing behind her like a shadow. She clutched at her chest, that same wheezing that she assumed came from her lungs filled the space around her. She thought of what Clarissa had said, about Mark enabling her. She resented being painted as some kind of addict, but as she watched him disappear, it was easier to see what she meant. It occurred to her in that flutter of a moment, that perhaps, when it came to Mark, she had held onto him like a trick mirror, reflecting the version he needed her to be back at her. And it made her think that while she was undeniably the better architect, perhaps Mark was the better illusionist. Convincing her that that reflection of herself was all she could ever be, then never taking responsibility for the consequences of his distortions of space.

VERSES ON ENTOMOLOGY

Lesser stag beetle
Dorcus parallelipipedus
30mm

Doomed to irrelevance by human categorisa-
tions, it is true that this beetle is smaller than
its famous cousin. But it is not less interesting
for it. Trees are at the centre of this beetle's
lifecycle. Both adults and larvae will be found
in the decaying wood of an ash or beech.
Adults mate there, planting their eggs in dead
cervices, as their larvae feed on the rotting
wood. Once wrapped in the flaking skin of a
dying bolster, they are able to repeat themselves, unspooling in the hollows of time.

It was another form of fortification. Another
form of hiding from faces, reflecting your
own limits, and your own helplessness.

Had Mark unspooled himself inside of her? Was she his survival strategy?

Unlike their better-appreciated cousins, who prefer the earthy undergrowth, they choose to feed on dead trees above the ground. They have given us all a gift; reminding us of the inevitability of death. That circular infinity that connects us all. Humans resent them for it. How dare he confront us with our own ending? So they moved the beetle linguistically out of sight, made it 'lesser.' Made it a shadow.

Did Jacky hate him? Hate him for making a home of her, and in doing so, confronting her with her own dependency? Had that made her squash him? Try to keep him small?
Mark was hiding, just like her. He'd found a skin, unfortunately it came in the shape of her body. But could she really blame him for looking to her, to something, for shelter?

The lesser stag was a dangerous beetle, bringing Jacky close to the edge of sympathy, and so, to the limits of her own defences.

13

Twitter was chaos. At first, Jacky thrived. Twitter was not unlike her own universe. Flat, homogenous, but charged. Tumultuous because there was just as much at stake. Within the confines of structured rules, the threat of losing loomed large.

Jacky had already adapted to these conditions. The key to facing the onslaught of critique was restricted motion; you could survive any storm if you clung to its centre. It was uncomfortable, but you'd survive, as long as you didn't stick your toe out too far. The threat of annihilation might surround you, the judgements, the people trying to suck you in. But the centre was a densely quiet place, a stable point held by surrounding chaos. She knew that, instinctively, and so she did everything she could to stay there.

Staying still required acceleration. Jacky knew what to do, or rather, she didn't think, didn't have time to. Her actions were reflexes. Circumventing consciousness, her body acted, fingers tweeting in a feedback loop evading thought. Visceral but disembodied, her limbs became an extension of that mechanism, a machine she inhabited but didn't control. Tap, click, buzz. Repeat.

Did she enjoy it? It was a complicated question. Mark would have told her she did. Maybe she did but not for reasons he could understand. She liked how it focused her mind. That familiar quiet, how in the fight for survival there was less time to think about death. She liked how it made her feel powerful, facing mortality in a head on struggle against the people who wanted to end her. The enemy had manifested. She didn't have to imagine the worst. That gave her peace. Their hatred openly on display. And she was still alive. She could survive that. To use the enemy's word: it was empowering. They'd have hated her for saying that.

First, she'd tried to lure the beast out of its cave. Succinct, and still cautious, prodding it with a verbal stick:

Jacky Mackenzie
Women aren't cattle.

The journalist responded immediately. Jacky was soothed by the pace of the web. Perhaps she'd been too quick to dismiss social media. It was, she had to admit, exhilarating.

Sally_Sacks
Cultural critic @The Times. All views my own.
Forget the entertainment business. Fascinating glimpse into a shadow-world of misogyny with the diva starchitect aka eugenicist @JackyMackenzie who sees no place for pregnant women in her build-ings, or in the world.

Jacky Mackenzie
I don't believe in milking women in back rooms like cows. Shoot me.

Then there was no activity for a while. She wasn't relieved. If she was honest, her pride was slightly hurt. She'd over-estimated her own fame. Had assumed that people would take an interest at least in the controversy. She threw her phone down on the bed, which she hadn't left all morning, feet growing sweaty and then crusty between the sheets as she'd downloaded and set up the app in a frustrated fury. Determined, somehow, to prove something to Mark. Either by destroying everything or surpassing his expectations, she wasn't sure. Whichever came first. She looked out the window and felt the pang of a pre-caffeine headache. She considered making a coffee and putting the whole thing out of her head for a while, an option she quickly dismissed as defeatist.

She dropped another pebble into the disquietingly quiet void:

Jacky MacKenzie
Did you know that rape tends to happen in dark corners?

She looked at the tweet she'd created, her name hovering over it like a foreign specimen. It was fascinating, this new form of spontaneous generation. Alive, and then instantly dead, always in need of replacing with something new. It was a beautiful pattern to her. A new trail of beetles in the ever-expanding taxonomy of herself. Only, of course, they, out there, had the power to end it all, not through hostility but neglect. She needed them to answer her.

She looked down at the tweet rapidly fading into the abyss. It glimmered like a dying star. Suddenly she saw in it the faint glimmer of redemption. A way to win over the critics who, despite their total lack of purchasing power, apparently, suddenly mattered.

Jacky MacKenzie
Rapists don't distinguish between lactation rooms
and seedy alleyways. Danger thrives in hidden
places.

She sighed into the pocket of sense she'd created, the chaos of her thoughts coalescing into the seedlings of a streamline. Suddenly, she was bursting with new life. She leapt from the bed, abandoned her phone, and returned to the drawing board she knew.

She spent the night sketching. She conjured new creatures, freakish offspring she intended to disown immediately. By the time the dew lit up the grass below the sardonically gentle baby blue of a new day's sky, she'd posted the first of her designs on Twitter.

Design 1. Featuring a revamped sketch of the now infamous university building. This image wasn't far from the original, still made of glass, only the sight-lines had been rearranged, the space divided into kaleidoscopic tunnels.

She posted the image with the caption: 'Out of sight out of mind? Not on my watch. Nowhere to hide in my buildings. Not even for rapists.'

Design 2. Featuring curved walls. The meeting of sides smoothed into continuous, rounded spaces. 'No dark corners in my buildings. That's why they're safe for women.'

Design 3. Featuring a set of stairs. The stairs were more like a series of landings, each of them sloped, awkwardly narrow, the rise between them smaller than average. Optimised for female feet. Designed to break the stride of the rapist pursuing his victim. 'Rape-proof stairs. A prototype.'

Jacky was pleased. She'd made her point eloquently. For a moment, she was hopeful that she'd done enough to at least placate her critics. But she was quickly faced with her societal disconnect. The scandal rippled. It pulled even the less volatile atoms into its broil. Even a few architects, usually such private creatures, poked their heads out to condemn her. That hurt her more than expected. She was totally alone. So be it.

Big-shot architect who prefers to remain anonymous:
Rape is not marketing fodder.

Jacky MacKenzie
At least I don't build phalluses that rape the sky.

Now that things were reaching new heights of absurdity, comedians heard their queue to take the stage.

Formerly famous comedian (recently cancelled):
I respect architects for their vision. Even more for
their sense of humour. Props to @JackyMacKenzie
for bringing back the rape joke.

Jacky laughed at that. Found herself cackling maniacally
into the echoey cavity of her empty house. She laughed
as her thumbs twitched and her heart raced. As the world
around her blurred. As she fell further down that nauseating
tunnel of nonsensical reality.

14

Jacky was an evolutionary impossibility. Maybe that had been part of Clarissa's fascination with her. How this twig-like woman with self-destructive tendencies stayed determinedly upright. How she kept going, frantically buzzing on the brink of death. It was fascinating, watching her fluctuate between inflated confidence and immobilising insecurity; the two logical poles of her world order. Clarissa only got to witness one extreme. Jacky turned to Mark when she was confident, to Clarissa was she was weak. That was the dance they did, the three of them.

Clarissa imagined how Mark would be hovering over the newspaper reports with a sense of schadenfreude. He enjoyed watching Jacky falter, she was sure of it, knowing Clarissa would pick up the pieces.

Clarissa had met up with Mark once. At a bar in Chelsea. Years ago. He'd come straight from work; she'd come straight from Jacky, which he knew. It was in the early days. Clarissa had just entered the scene, was still adjusting to the role of being Jacky's emotional crutch, and Mark, already a weathered workhorse, was curious about her. That's what she thought, innocently curious, just as she was childishly curious about the male lover Clarissa would be compared to.

'I'm completely fine with all this, I want you to know that. I'm really not jealous at all.'

Clarissa believed him. Even then, she sensed that any possessiveness he felt for Jacky, or affection for that matter, was secondary to his self-interest. Even back then, that was clear to her.

'I can see that.'

'Thing is, you're still in the honeymoon phase. And you don't work with her.'

'You haven't done too badly out of all that.'

Mark looked that city version of rugged. Shirt crumpled after a workday, five o'clock shadow, tired eyes. He looked soft to Clarissa, a clean urban masculinity that came across entitled.

'It's a lot sometimes, you'll see.' He took another sip and glanced at her with his head tilted back arrogantly. His default mode, she would come to see. 'She likes you a lot, I can tell. More than she'd ever admit.'

'We've got a good thing going.' Clarissa said coolly. She wasn't going to let Mark into their sacred space. The two relationships could never touch. She knew that instinctively.

'It's good to know that she has you, is all I'm saying. Sometimes it feels like we're in over our heads, the two of us.'

Clarissa felt her stomach contract then. The sense that she'd been picking at a loose thread of a tightly woven tapestry. The fear that it might unravel irrevocably. She was scared. She'd sensed that darkness in Jacky. A daunting black hole that swallowed surrounding matter. Not like the knots of her past that just needed patient tending. From the moment Clarissa had found Jacky on the edge of the pier, glaring dangerously into the foaming water, she saw in her the capacity for destruction.

The truth was that it had been more than a petty curiosity about the competition that had led her to meet with Mark. If she was honest, she'd been hoping for an excuse to meet him from the moment she'd learned of his existence. She'd been hoping for a chance to ask him for the truth about Jacky. She trusted Mark to know the truth better than Jacky herself. How fucked up was that? She berated herself for that failure of trust. What kind of a premise for a relationship was that? All it had taken was one text to entice her. She deserved Jacky's noncommittal dependency, because, really, Jacky had always risked more. Clarissa had never been all-in. She was as bad as Mark, a feeling that was already latent but lurking when she'd first met him. Even back then, it made her crabby.

'You're as bad as she is. In over your heads? Like this is some kind of Great Roman Empire you're building. You have a business. You could stop any day. It's not out of your control. Take responsibility, for god's sake.'

Mark's face contracted, his tired eyes narrowed into slits. 'You'll see.'

Clarissa took a breath.

'I'm confused about why you asked me here.'

Mark's face relaxed. He liked this question, probably because it assumed he was an intentional kind of person.

'Look, I can tell you've already decided to make me the dickhead here. I don't know what Jacky's told you, she's become so bitter. She never used to gossip.' Clarissa watched him darken then quickly recover himself.

'I care about her, though. I just want to make sure that we have some ground rules. These unconventional relationships, they need rules, or people get hurt.'

'Well, yeah.' Clarissa raised a lesbian eyebrow at the cis male mansplaining relationships to her.

'I don't think she really understands the implications. She always over-estimates herself. Which is great, it makes her fearless, means she'll take risks. But she gets whiplash. I just want to make sure she doesn't –'

He stopped, trying to find the words, Clarissa's eyebrow climbing higher, daring him to say something infantilising, condescending, sexist.

'Mark, what is it you want?'

'I just want you to know how she can be. So, you're prepared.'

Clarissa watched him shift towards the edge of his sleek hard wooden stool and it dawned on her.

'You want me to pick up the pieces if it all goes to shit.'

'Well it wouldn't be all on me, would it?'

Clarissa understood suddenly how lonely Jacky had been. She leaned back, took him in, this image of a person, slight like Jacky, but formless compared to her.

'Honestly, this feels weird.' They were speaking in hypotheticals, in potential futures, and at the same time, Clarissa knew just then, manifesting them. This is what Mark wanted. Something shifted inside her, the familiar interior rearranging to accommodate others' needs.

Mark straightened in his seat, pulling at his trouser legs, revealing paisley socks at the end of his twigs.

'I just wanted to make sure we were on the same page.'

'And now we are. Now I know how committed you are to making this work.'

His face twitched again. 'Let's get the bill.' He was flustered. His hand flicked up and a waitress immediately caught sight of the gesture. Mark wasn't used to being left hanging.

'I just wanted to meet you,' he said now that he'd had time to recover. He looked so pathetic, like a boy in a fancy-dress suit. Clarissa hated that she felt sorry for him. She understood Jacky better now, the resentment she felt, how she hated herself for loving him while he took it all for granted.

'I'm going to take care of her,' Clarissa heard herself say. The words reverberated through her body reminding her of all the empty space she contained. In that moment, she had to say it. She would protect Jacky from this grasshopper man. Whether Jacky needed it or not, the choice seemed between two opposing influences, and she was sure her own would be better for Jacky. That's how she justified it all. That conversation in the dark corner at the back of a swanky bar, conspiring like parents about the best way to 'handle' Jacky. About how to set 'boundaries' and 'manage expectations'. And, should push come to shove, about who would abandon her first.

Mark looked up at her, suddenly energised. 'That's all I wanted to hear.'

The boy jumped up from his seat. He searched the room for a waitress and spotted one at the bar near the door.

'I'll get it on the way out.' And he turned away, with a youthful spring in his step.

A Scarab Where the Heart Should Be

Clarissa sat staring after him, at the boy in his costume, paying for things the way he'd learned men did. She shrugged. There was no point. He wasn't the one she needed to save.

15

Mark was cleaning the apartment. The mess had amassed to a natural crescendo. Now it was time to clean. Jacky would never understand. It wasn't that he let chaos swamp him, just that he trusted natural cycles. Moods came and went. You just had to ride the wave. She could learn from him, about letting go of order every once in a while. It probably would have helped them. They should have planned that in.

It was all quite spiritual, really, his newfound self-understanding. Most of it came from techno. From those moments, in the early hours of a rave, when he looked up and glimpsed a higher truth. Something in the light of laser beams piercing puffs of multicoloured smoke cracked open his tight and anxious chest. When that opening coincided with the drop, it was fucking transcendent. Goosebumps, the works. He could *feel* again. Jacky's voice, entirely gone, he'd surrender to the beat that was his truth. He'd rediscover his natural rhythm. His instincts restored, he could *trust* again. No need for the hyper-vigilance that came with sneaking around. He was present. He could trust the music to carry him, from the depths of big blobs of sound, back to a safe plateau, where he'd coast for a while, waiting for the next devastatingly beautiful moment.

It was lucky that he felt so impelled to clean that day, the day before he departed for Stockholm. This way he'd come home to a clean flat. It was just business; no raves planned this time. But other important developments. It was good to be getting into the right headspace.

Techno had a guiding wisdom. Anything it hadn't taught him was a reflection of his own limitations. Techno was infinite. It would help him embrace the cycles of home maintenance too. He blasted his latest mix on his Bose speakers and set to work. *Just a spoonful of sugar*, he chuckled, hoover in hand, drawing clear trails in the sugardust on the floorboards. Progress was quick; the place was pretty much cleaning itself. He was enjoying himself. Just him, in his rubber gloves, head bopping, fist-pumping his way around the apartment. Sliding across the way in his neon socks. He was losing himself to the process. He even whipped out his signature move, always a sign of immersion, a really cool circular fist-pump, where he'd slowly swivel around in a circle with his eyes closed, totally in tune with the vibe. Those were the moments.

Of course, it wasn't quite as good as the real deal. At a rave, he'd be surrounded by kindred spirits. He was missing his people; the Swedes got him. He didn't have to explain himself there. How to be socially-minded. How to be a decent human. He was supposed to be English but rave culture had made him see that he'd always been an outsider at home. It helped him understand why he'd gravitated towards Jacky. He shuddered at what a cliché they were, bonding over their shared outsider status. On the surface of it you'd never have guessed, he didn't struggle getting people to like him like *she* did. But it had always felt like a game with them. He had to guard himself against their rampant small-mindedness. The Brits, he now realised, had a self-interested national mentality. All they knew was righteous indignation and co-dependence. Someone's existence was either offensive or indispensable to them. People stuck together like miserable, needy amoebas. So underdeveloped in their individuality. The Swedes had shown him the meaning of real partnership. What he had with Jacky was a poor replica. All they'd done was build a different kind of cage.

It's not that he'd learnt nothing from the relationship. There had been challenges that had pre-empted some considerable personal growth. Clarissa coming into the picture had made him take a good close look at the state of his self-esteem. When they'd agreed to an open relationship, he'd never imagined Jacky would find anyone. There had always been this implicit understanding between them that she was impossible. That she was lucky to have found a human to handle her alien tendencies. It had been a shock, but he'd handled it graciously. He'd even met up with her, he'd given his blessing. It had been such a dopamine burst, being so selfless.

It had been more challenging than expected. At first, he thought it would help that Clarissa wasn't a man. But that, it turned out, only complicated the sense of rivalry between them. It was confusing. He almost wanted her to be attractive so he could contain her with his own desire, but there was something about her size and demeanour that made that impossible for him. So he was forced to take her in, to sit across from her and let her exist. It was awkward. But he got through it.

He'd persevered, and his reward was liberation. He'd transcended first the challenges, then their relationship. Jacky still needed him. That sucked for her. But he was learning how to be without her. It was a surprising turn of events, the extent of his own personal growth amazed him, too. He hadn't expected to progress this quickly. It was difficult to imagine what it meant for the rest of his life, or what it meant for Jacky's. It was intense, the thought of walking out on her after years of building her up, not knowing how she'd cope. For all the thrill of his newfound strength, the discordant drone of guilt was difficult to ignore. He dismissed it as his former consciousness trying to drag him back. But it was undeniable. The pitchiness of conscience, and the power of the beat. Both were true, yet, together, they were paradoxical.

Mark didn't know how to make sense of it. So he danced.

16

The university she had so generously made refence to in her numerous interviews severed their contract after the Twitter storm. Jacky didn't care, that's what she told herself. The online spats had generated a new wave of online media attention. A slew of video and podcast interview requests. The degree of public interest in architecture was well and truly unprecedented. Although it was hard to see how it would be good for business. Jacky watched as her public persona crystalised. A stream of comments placing her in a lineage of cold, heartless women, an eclectic cast ranging from Thatcher to J.K. Rowling. She watched as they undressed her, stripping away her layers – everything she did, everything she was, how they tore it away and politicised it. Her clothes were fascist, her earrings conservative, her posture elitist.

In the end, they talked the most about the phrase she'd used in that first interview.

There was an inexplicable fascination with the idea of the 'lactation room'. The clunky phrase describing women as cattle had become the rallying point of her opposition, the irony of them acting like sheep in doing so totally lost on them.

They probably liked it because it allowed them to steer clear of less palatable subjects. Rape left a bitter taste on people's twittering tongues. That is to say, they were scared, as always, to stick their necks out.

'Lactation room' became a word of the year. It was everywhere, in the bold type-font of newspaper headlines, in Twitter feuds and TikTok videos of women proudly and defiantly squeezing their breasts as if milking them. 'Milk tits not the patriarchy,' they captioned. It took a few weeks for some diligent reporters to add to the list of allegations, unearthing the lower profile pro bono projects Jacky had rejected in favour of highly visible ventures. STARCHITECT TOO POSH TO PUSH FOR SOCIAL JUSTICE. Women working office jobs in the skyscrapers Jacky had designed began resigning publicly.

And where the fuck was Mark?

He was posting photos of the building site of some project in Sweden Jacky had missed or wasn't involved with – who knew. Who knew what nest eggs he was hoarding to save himself while he fed her to the wolves. All this could have been too much for most people to take. But Jacky...

She responded the way any villain worth their salt would. By perfecting her look. In the tall bedroom mirror, she modelled a new pair of bug-eyed sunglasses. She propped the dark pointed black collars of her jackets up and swept her angular fringe decisively across her face. Nothing much changed, really, she just turned it all up a notch, enough to make the whole thing highly intentional. She had stopped defending herself. Once satisfied, she picked up her phone.

She found an especially silly photo of Mark, dazzling whites gleaming, big head stuffed into a silly round helmet, showing him in animated conversation with a mixed group of executives and construction workers. Such a man of the people. She posted it, with the caption:

.@MarkPrice on the site of a Scandinavian venture. @BeetleInc supports the values of the world's most progressive countries.

A subtle announcement of the company's rebranding. If Mark wanted to distance himself, so be it. MacKenzie and Price would go with him. It would live on, but in a different guise. She would wear the company the way she wore everything she did. Defiantly. As the face and founder of the singular and visionary Beetle Inc.

She watched her comment, thrown like a grenade, but really, testing for a sign of life. She watched the comment beat, swell, contract, once, twice. Then it was gone.

He'd deleted it. The fucker. He'd stomped on her frantic, pixelated heart. It was brutal. Without a moment's hesitation, he'd severed their digital connection. Like squashing the bug of an @-sign in cyberspace. Of all the people who could have annihilated her with their neglect, it was Mark who had cyber-killed her. She hated him for it. She also hated Twitter for it. This was what was wrong with the world. How these platforms, these people on these platforms, reduced relations to something so insubstantial they could be severed into meaningless fractals with a single tap. She hated Mark and she hated the world. But only one of them might care.

VERSES ON ENTOMOLOGY

Deathwatch beetle
Xestobium rufovillosum
5-9mm

Beware of the Deathwatch beetle!

Produces a tapping noise in the middle of the night heralding tragedy. Haunting, however, is a subsidiary concern, given wood-boring causes major damage in houses.

Although of course, decay is a form of haunting. That life festering in the shadows of our homes.

The Deathwatch beetle knows how we humans fear the dark.

It takes us a while, to make the connection, between the unassuming exterior of an unremarkable visitor – drab, plain, and hairy –

and the danger he contains. How he gradually tunnels his way through our supporting beams. Until one day, there is nothing left. And we realise that we'd lost sight of our houses, fallen prey to this little devil's wicked diversion. Distracted, as we always are, by sounds in the night.

Men like Mark work insidiously like that.

PART 2

FISSURES

17

Clarissa had taken her boat to the lighthouse. At night and alone, as she liked to. She set out at dusk so that she'd arrive when the sun had set completely, docking in the total darkness, when the light at the top of the tower was the brightest. It wasn't advisable, of course. She never told anyone she'd left, and so her departure always came with the risk of her disappearing, of being swallowed by the sea.

Drowning was just the tip of the iceberg when it came to the ocean's power to render you insignificant. She knew that from the portion of her life she had spent out at sea. Never all of it, of course, never the way of the diehards, the generations before her who sailed to get somewhere. She'd dabbled, for leisure, making a performance of exploration, always with a safety net, never truly cutting ties. But she'd dabbled consistently and she'd seen a few things. The magic you see through salt crystals glazing your eyeballs. She'd always thought it was misogyny that had made the sailors of yesteryear see mermaids. Now she knew it was salt that made you see the things you feared and loved merged into one.

Out there in the thick of voluminous grey was the only place she let her torment rise. Her torment was a mermaid.

Jacky. Frail on the surface, dangerous underneath. It wasn't Jacky's fault she was deceptive. She was just a reflection of Clarissa's own chimeric insides. Clarissa, the woman who denied her shadowy past, her shadowy feelings, her shadowy needs. That way of being made anyone dangerous. She made herself the impenetrable rock for people to lash their tails against.

She was sturdy. Her body was a manifestation of who she was. But sometimes she wondered if it was actually the other way round. People telling her she was strong, people always interpreting what she did as a sign of strength. They wouldn't have seen weakness in her if she'd broken down in front of them. She looked big, and she looked strong. And so she had to be. And the bigger and stronger she was to them, the smaller her presence became. Inoffensive, that was her way. Her soul was as withered as Jacky's body. Worn-out remains from a life of pandering. But no one would have known.

The way Clarissa was with Jacky was weak. The way she let Jacky treat her was weak.

In her resentful moments Clarissa told herself that Jacky had got the better deal – she'd found a buttress twice the size of her. It was all very one-sided. Then she reminded herself how Jacky was the only one risking anything. Jacky was the centre, but she was also the human sacrifice. She and Mark were her buttresses, but in the end, they could pull away. They had practiced steadiness that would carry them into another arrangement. Jacky was totally dependent on their very particular construction for support. She would collapse without them. Clarissa had her freedom, she always reassured herself in the moments that Jacky turned to Mark. She would survive regardless. Nothing but the ocean could destroy her.

Her boat hit the lighthouse's pedestal and she threw out a snaky rope, her muscles taut and dangerous as she tightened it. She had the power to draw herself in, or release. But for how long? The real shackle, of course, was never going to be Jacky, but the other buttress in their constellation. Mark. Mark would pull away, leaving Clarissa solely responsible. That move would bind her to Jacky. She wouldn't have it in her to walk away. The ocean was the only place she could let that twisted irony sink in. The irony of relinquishing her freedom to a man.

The boat steadied, strapped into place. Clarissa hopped easily across the gap of shadowy water, her feet landing on the rock with a dense thud. She saw things clearly from her island in the night. She and Mark had decided Jacky's fate together. She'd given him permission to give up, because it made her feel powerful. She plodded across the rock towards the patch of grass that marked her usual spot and sat down, settling her gaze on the silhouette of her boat against the chalky sky. They had stripped Jacky down and turned her into brittle plywood. She had to live with that. She had done it to protect herself. Her own freedom, at the cost of Jacky's. Now she realised she'd sacrificed her own.

She could find a way to reconcile herself with her fate. As long as Jacky never knew about the decisions that had been made for her. You only needed the illusion of choice to be free. At least Jacky could be free.

A Scarab Where the Heart Should Be

Clarissa looked up at the lighthouse and imagined its keeper, a character worthy of the post. A drunkard, of course, definitely a man. Men were allowed to be lonely and sad, she'd settled for lonely and helpful. She knew in reality the lighthouse was automated. No one lived there. Machines had replaced the people emitting guiding lights for others. People like her eventually became obsolete, forgotten only in the moments that we thought to remember them at all. And that was fine, Clarissa expected it, had limited herself to being an invisible presence, or visible absence, she no longer knew which. She no longer really knew what she had chosen for, although she was determined to believe that she had chosen. She sat there on that island and imagined the rest of her life. How she would retire eventually, sink into it, probably tending to her boat alongside old crusty sailors who didn't want her in their country. All this while dragging Jacky along, unless Mark decided to bail, in which case Jacky might remember her, might even choose her and turn to the lighthouse, only to realise that her lover was as tinny and unfeeling, as void as a machine.

VERSES ON ENTOMOLOGY

Cockchafer
Melolontha melolontha
2.5-3cm

Long known to be a pest, the English none-
theless claimed the cockchafer with their
culture. Cockchafer means 'big beetle' in Old
English, but it is more commonly known as
the 'May bug'. *Cockchafers* are large, noisy
beetles that fly around at dusk and warm
evenings, making a noisy hum as they dart
through the air with pointed posteriors.
Frightening to some, but actually harmless.

The humming, in fact, is a distraction from a
much more insidious affront. As people swat
at adult bugs on warm summer evenings, as
they shelter their children from frightening
appearances, the maybug launches her true
affront. The long and pointed segment at the
end of a cockchafer's abdomen is called the

pygidium and, while it resembles a weapon, it is actually a tool used by females to lay eggs into the ground. These fat, creamy-white grubs with brown heads devour plant roots in the soil. This is how she attacks the crops that sustain us. This is how the cockchafer leaves her mark on the world. Her attack is on the lifeblood, not the beating heart. Her aims are intergenerational.

The beetles were closing in on her. At first, they had opened her world up. They had helped her expand into a new realm of kinship. They'd given her a glimmer of a new kind of freedom, less about streamlining, more of belonging. A vision that reduced her influence in the grander scheme of things, and let her be a creature. But now the beetles were moving in, circling her like the people she knew, threatening to displace her needs with their own.

Clarissa worked like a cockchafer. She buried her larvae in Jacky's life, unleashing doubts and questions that unfurled with dangerous potential. Questions that gnawed at her roots. That changed her fundamentally.

Challenging everything Jacky was. Making her creaturely in all the wrong ways. Susceptible to human delusions. Distracted by the appearance of things. Prey to simple tricks. And, once again, ever so disconcertingly, to sympathy.

There it was again. The cockchafer distracted her, illuminating another being's survival mechanism, making them appear more like her. Clarissa, like Jacky, had found a skin to hide in. Her larvae were her defence against decay. In human terms, words containing hope. Those words were dangerous eggs. They drew Jacky away from her streamline. And yet, she understood why Clarissa needed them. Jacky's own fear coexisted with that understanding in a new frightening complexity.

18

Clarissa was right. Jacky had spent the night thinking about the story, about the mother who had lost her son. She'd been thinking about that and how she was on her own now, and still, as ever, misunderstood. And suddenly Clarissa's meaning dawned on her. It was the kind of meaning that comes to you by osmosis, like the salt on the back of a battered hump of cod.

She saw it now. She'd been neglecting a whole dimension of her experience. She thought about what she'd told the journalists about her ovaries. About them being too streamlined to have children. Those comments were connected, somehow, to Clarissa telling her that she wasn't living. And they were connected to Mark always accusing her of thinking she was better than everyone. It was all pointing in the same direction. So simple, it was almost streamlined.

The thing was, endangered species didn't reproduce. Jacky had been too preoccupied with survival, with securing shelter and security in a world that was hostile to her. She'd sacrificed her body to the pursuit of a different kind of legacy because she'd had no choice. The meanings and answers people had designed didn't make sense to her. They had evolved for an entirely different, tangentially related, remote cousin in the animal kingdom. She'd needed a house before she could build a family. She'd had to birth a new world order that would welcome her kind, before she could think about populating the world with more of her.

She'd taken her architectural gestation seriously. Jacky had always been fiercely competitive about subordinating her body to her will. She'd learnt how to do it at university. The professors applauded her efforts. One night in the first year, she'd accidently sliced the top off her finger, a clean swipe with a cutting machine in the midst of one of the all-nighters that sorted the mediocre students from the good. She'd stymied the bleeding with a bandage but the blood had seeped through. She'd watched crimson blotches stain the page of her sketches as her hand worked out the details of her design, splattering the edges with the more expressive flicks of her pencil. She'd presented the work the following day, black coffee dilating the veins that held the blood still coursing through her twitching body. Hands shaking (from caffeine, not nerves), she'd presented her design to the room. 'Excuse the blood,' she'd said. But she wasn't sorry, she was defiant. She got a First, of course.

It irritated her when others outperformed her. A classmate cut into her leg. Jacky hadn't witnessed the incident but she did watch resentfully as the girl had stuffed her wound with coffee grinds from the kitchen, the smell of espresso forever corrupted by the metal scent of someone else's efforts. It threw her off, seeing that. Her work had suffered. She decided after that day to work in isolation whenever she could, abandoning the well-equipped studio for empty classrooms in off-peak hours. It was worth the material inconvenience because it elevated her. Away from the deceptive resonance of other people's struggles, she was limitless.

In the past Jacky had, admittedly, looked on biological reproduction with disdain. Children were a consolation prize for people who had wasted their lives. They told themselves that children could go and do the living for them. Children who 'made it all worthwhile'. Their children would simply replicate their parents' unoriginal nonexistence. They wouldn't grow or innovate. They'd do the same hapless hiding, have more children to assuage their own inherited complacency. And so the spiral of degradation would go on, as humanity bred into the void of a lifecycle they didn't know how to use.

It must have been Clarissa's influence that had made her view herself with newfound understanding. It must have been her persistent doctrine of self-compassion that made her see that she wasn't opposed to children, just not *safe* enough to consider them. That she'd fled from her heart to her head. But that in the safety of the new world she was creating, she could, perhaps, eventually, possibly imagine considering it.

And with all that in mind, it occurred to Jacky that there might be more ways than one to streamline her ovaries.

19

Jacky drove to the clinic for her 3pm appointment in London. She stopped at a café on the corner on the way and ordered a croissant with her espresso. Not at all paleo but it seemed like a thing a woman concerned with her fertility would do. For her first croissant in a decade, it was disappointingly dry.

She then made her way to the building – Edwardian – and took a seat in the waiting room on the lower ground floor. The space had been decorated in a poor imitation of Japanese minimalism that people associated with scientific prowess. Blue floor lights illuminated cheap laminate and chipboard chairs. The walls were, predictably, white. The only feature of the underground room she liked was the long angular window at the top of the wall, peeking out on the bottom of a cherry blossom tree, the narrow section turning the protruding roots into the room's branches. Jacky focused on that slice of light until a woman dressed in a lab coat appeared in the doorway and, with a gleaming smile, invited Ms MacKenzie to follow her.

'It's Mrs,' Jacky said, somewhat defensively. It was true, purely for legal reasons. She didn't usually like to talk about it. But something about the place made her feel she had to legitimate herself conventionally.

Laminate gave way to linoleum. Jacky followed the woman in the lab coat down a narrow corridor as she tried to blur out the haunting images of ecstatic blonde women cooing over angelic babies on the walls. She had to work hard in the face of the flashy-toothed parents, to remember that her ovaries didn't belong to them. She focused on the light at the end of the narrow corridor, at that open office door.

'Here we are.'

Sweet euphoria, a room full of windows. Jacky fixed her gaze on the pavement outside, at a plane tree, anything to avoid the harrowing framed image of the same baby, replicated four times with four different facial expressions on the wall in front of her.

'Sit down, please.'

Jacky stood still, unable to drag her eyes back.

'I know it's a lot.' The doctor gestured at the terrifying picture. 'Makes it look like a sweetshop. Just pick the colour you want. People honestly think it works like that.'

Jacky inspected the woman. The tinge of cynicism was reassuring, but in a place like this, she had to remain cautious.

'They're trying to sell the dream, I suppose. You can't blame them, really. It's a daunting process. People need a bit of inspiration.'

Jacky's scepticism returned. This doctor didn't know who she was dealing with.

'I don't need inspiring, thank you.'

She looked at Jacky, eyes sad, but unapologetic, dyssynchronous with the words she spoke.

'Of course, I wasn't suggesting –'

'I'm highly self-motivated.'

'Fantastic. That'll help you in this process.'

Jacky looked at the doctor. She really didn't have a clue. These people were used to selling childbearing to the dominant species. People who bought dreams because they didn't have their own. She'd let Clarissa corrupt her with her fairy tale thinking. It was preposterous, to think, even with all the scientific assistance in the world, that Jacky could squeeze herself into the mould of a childbearing woman.

The doctor smiled again, oblivious to Jacky's distrust of her. For a moment Jacky imagined how good it would feel to trust doctors unquestioningly. The prospect was dizzying. She sat down and clutched onto the metal handles on the flimsy polypropylene chair, steadying her swaying torso. The doctor watched silently.

Jacky swallowed to lubricate her vocal cords. It was important that she found her voice now. *She* would determine the agenda for their meeting.

'I've asked you here today to discuss my options with me.'

The doctor stifled a grin. Jacky noticed. This was the kind of inconsistency she found in most people. Cracks in their professionalism, an irritating transparency that exposed their weakness. She was laughing at her, the way everyone did. She knew what she was thinking. 'What a character.' She would tell her colleagues about her in their lunchbreak.

'We can definitely do that.' That calmed Jacky down, but only slightly. 'I'll just ask you a few personal questions, if that's OK, just to build a picture. Then we'll explore our options.'

Our. She was on Jacky's side. Of course. That was how they talked. But it occurred to Jacky in that moment that she'd never explored 'our' options with Mark. They'd just decided on one. They hadn't really explored anything since their undergraduate days, when they'd searched the city for new forms. After that, their creativity had stagnated. The dizziness returned. A gargling, choking noise emerged from the depths of her throat. The doctor couldn't have missed it but she didn't react. Instead, she turned to her laptop screen.

'How long have you been trying to conceive?'

Jacky returned to the present.

'I haven't tried,' she said, curtly, emphasis on 'tried' implying that she wasn't someone who tried, but someone who succeeded.

'I see. I'm sorry, I assumed. May I ask if you're in a relationship?'

'That's irrelevant.'

The doctor's hands slipped from her keyboard.

'This is all perfectly fine. We welcome women at all stages of their fertility journey here.'

Jacky opened her mouth to unclench her jaw which had instinctively locked at the words, 'fertility journey'.

The doctor's fingers returned to the keyboard. 'Is it egg freezing you're interested in?'

She'd lost focus, a momentary lapse in concentration was all it took. Now the doctor was pushing her down some prototypical path for prototypical complacency.

'This isn't what I came for.' The doctor looked at her. Stupid, and befuddled.

'These are just standard questions, so that I can give you the right information.'

'Can you just tell me know how long it will take?'

She nodded.

'That's a good question. I suppose it's not just a question of time. It's the toll it takes on your body too. It's physically very taxing. That's another consideration.'

She looked at Jacky, expecting some kind of retort. But Jacky was silent now, interest piqued by the prospect of a physical challenge.

'I suppose what we're trying to do, although it's a difficult process, is to get your body working for you, not against you.'

Jacky nodded vigorously.

'Is this the right time for you? Are you in the right place, financially, and otherwise?'

There it was again, that gargling noise. The sound of her deep and irremediable despair. The doctor looked at her, face acknowledging the unseemly belch this time with a stifled flinch. Jacky wanted to explain it to her. But she found herself, as usual when it came to these natural urges, void of an explanation.

'I'm not sure,' she told her, defeated.

'That's fine.' The doctor smiled, in a way that came close to not being condescending.

'Any fertility issues in your family?'

This woman was playing with her, folding her like origami, building her trust, then crumpling her in the grasp of her fist.

'I don't like to talk about family.'

The doctor raised an eyebrow that same way anyone asking Jacky about her family always did. Judgement tinged with fear at the psychopath with no past.

'I see.' She sighed. 'Have you been tested for early onset menopause? It's genetic. Maybe that'll influence your decision?'

'That won't be necessary.'

She should have known they'd fail her. They'd given up before they'd even begun; already justifying their scientific limitations. This was a space beyond the streamline. When it came to bending the body their will, this was the best most people could do.

'You want to take the pressure off making the decision. I understand that, but most people like to be informed, to understand their options, should they decide.'

Jacky looked at her, at this woman in her lab coat, radiating white. She focused on the gap between two of the buttons of her white coat to see what she was wearing underneath. Jacky almost envied her for her prescribed uniform. *She* had had to invent her own. For a moment she thought she could glimpse the V-neck of a knit the colour of menstrual blood.

The doctor slid a brochure across the desk.

'I think perhaps you need time to think.'

'I didn't say that.'

'Alright.' She smiled again. She just kept smiling. Like Jacky didn't know that behind that façade this woman was as cold the clinic's vats gathering human eggs like frogspawn.

The woman was trying very hard now, Jacky could tell, to maintain an air of levity. They held eye contact for a while. The doctor's irises the iciest of blue, and Jacky's, she'd been told by lovers and fearful enemies, oily shades of copper.

'I just want to freeze my eggs. I want to freeze them because I think the possibility of a child with some of my genetic material is worth putting on ice. I don't see myself as responsible for birthing that potential reality. Only for creating the possibility. That's where I stand, and I wanted you to help me. That is, as I understand it, what I will be paying you to do.'

'A potential donation to a couple in need. That's lovely.'

She sighed.

'I didn't say that. It's about me. My life. It's about me claiming my potentiality.' Jacky smiled as she thought of the stretch of space and time between Mark and Clarissa; a beautiful matrix of possibilities.

'Look, you want to keep your options open, I understand that. It's a perfectly legitimate motivation. As women we're often told it's not, that it's our duty to have children while we can.'

Jacky tried to catch another glimpse of that red jumper as the doctor repeated herself. The doctor caught her looking, misinterpreting her wandering eyes for a different kind of violation. She pulled her coat closed.

'But I will say that there are plenty of women hoping to continue their fertility journey with us. They do need the space.'

'At these prices I'm sure capacity isn't an issue.'

'Perhaps you'd be happier at a lab that just does storage.'

'You mean you'd be happier.'

She smiled, again, eyes now spurting ice like frosty tentacles. This, Clarissa, is what comes of 'speaking your truth'. Frostbite.

'I wouldn't say that, no.'

'Fine.' Jacky shot up, taking one last peak at the bloody red covering the doctor's breasts, just to stoke the fire. Then she walked out without saying goodbye. She had to admit that she felt rejected. The ice-woman's questions had set her up to sound unconvincing, and worse – unconvinced. Like she didn't know what she wanted at all. Jacky strode past the receptionist, ignoring a high-pitched voice asking her if she wanted to make a 'follow-up appointment'. It was just a strategy, a marketing trick, for people who needed to pay for answers.

20

Jacky made her way to a café next to the one that had provided her with the stale croissant. She wouldn't entertain underwhelming pastries with the widening holes in the stretched dough of her existence. This café suited her better. Metallic benches, white walls. Her kind of clinical. She walked in and squeezed herself onto a bench behind a small square table, taking pleasure in tucking the pleats of her coat in, arranging her narrow satchel bag so that it sat perfectly parallel beside her own compact body. She ordered an espresso. Black. Nothing else. And pulled out her iPad.

Jacky had stuck her foot out. Just for a moment, she'd left the eye of her storm, veered into the chaos where most people live. No wonder she was dizzy. She needed to steady herself. The moment called for acceleration.

What she needed was a no-frills egg freezing facility. A place that wouldn't ask questions and just got the job done. She would find a lab that offered storage, just storage, not fertility treatment or endless discussions about bodily processes that she was paying people to render irrelevant. She would store her eggs, like she'd intended, and her eggs wouldn't be used for anything or become anyone. They'd just sit there, indefinitely, in glassy ice. As her perfectly designed legacy.

Perhaps it was all the disorienting talk about children, Jacky would never usually have allowed her focus to be interrupted, but for whatever reason, as she opened her web browser to search for a clinic, she felt impelled to google Mark. It hadn't occurred to her before, with all the publicity pressure, to see if anyone had bothered to write about him. Perhaps it had been hubris, perhaps self-preservation. Perhaps she was about to find out.

She selected the first article from her search results and scanned the page. The usual preamble about her stream-lined aesthetic, about her 'controversial' opinions along with oblique references to her unlikeable personality. But following that, the piece took an unruly turn, and shifted focus to her partner.

> Mark Price is the shadow to Mackenzie's public persona. Unlike his long-term partner, he chooses to keep a low profile, spending much of his time in Sweden, a place to which he is drawn, he told *The Angle*, not just for its architectural aesthetic, which undeniably resonates with his new firm's style, but also for its work ethic. 'We're trialling a four-day work week with amazing results,' he said. With a politics of caring in stark contrast to Mackenzie's, some sources have suggested that his move to start his own firm is also a

personal departure, speculation on which he refused to comment.

His new firm. Her espresso arrived. She looked up at the bearded youth wearing a leather apron and imagined the satisfaction that would come from confusing the alien species across from her with the enigma of a void in the place of her head. How it would be for her mouth to swallow her face like a vortex. Her cheeks twitched at the thought of it. The barista was too blasé to notice her facial contortions. He placed the glass cup on a glass saucer on the table and turned away.

The moment called for acceleration. Jacky replaced the words 'Mark Price' with the less daunting, 'egg freezing clinic London' in the search bar. One way or another, her eggs would need to be frozen. If Mark was plotting to exit their relationship, all the more reason to consolidate her legacy some other way. If it wasn't true, it would serve as a reminder not to rely on mortals for meaning.

She scrolled resolutely through the search results, amassing tabs, assessing the various clinics' offerings. She was moving swiftly, making a final selection of clinics she would proceed to call, one by one, to deduce whether they'd accommodate her worldview. She was making progress but it cost her a momentous effort. A wound had opened up in her, now throbbing with infection, sending pangs of doubt through her torso to the tips of her extremities. Doubts that took the form of comparison. She was falling, despite herself, into the trap that the journalists had set for her. They were trying to get to her, through him, to provoke her and generate more human interest. It was all a ploy to get to her.

Contradictory thoughts were starting to cause turbulence in her system. It made sense. That he was starting his own company. It explained why he hadn't reacted to her Beetle Inc tweet. If it wasn't true, he would have called her to tell her that. He was skulking. It explained his behaviour over the past months. It also explained their employees' behaviour – CC-ing him into all their correspondence with her, that is, when they bothered to reply to any of her emails. She'd thought of it as a new generation's collective incompetency. Now she saw that Mark had probably poached them, or at least turned them against her. They were either on their way out, or they were phasing her out. She wasn't sure which, what, where, how. Subordination, she was discovering, was hugely disorientating.

What else had he not told her? What else had he done to betray their transparency? Despite all her openness. She'd always been honest about Clarissa, but he'd always clung onto that something of his own. Openness to him meant escape, always had.

The truth was, he couldn't hack it. He'd never understood the sacrifice he was making. He wasn't used to sacrificing like that. Things came easily to him. He had no experience of the tearing away of tissue, the severing of parts of yourself. He didn't understand the ruthlessness streamlining demanded. Jacky did. That's why she was the face of the firm, and he knew it. Jacky *was* their dream. People sensed in her the total absence of doubt. How could she doubt when her entire self was streamlined to eliminate such inauthenticity? All of that seemed 'excessive' to Mark. Which it would be to someone who was used to flailing loose-limbed through life. Following, always following, but never committed. He'd use that word, more and more, 'this is getting excessive,' he'd say. The word-choice was a painful jab to her lean and tender heart. An excess of streamlining? An excessiveness in that process that was, by definition, the ridding of excess? It was oxymoronic. He had become oxymoronic. That kind of convolution could only be the beginning of the end.

Somehow, she'd ended up alone. In the face of her openness, he'd kept his hidden life. He'd clutched dishonestly onto that something of his own. He'd lured her into a shared space but there'd been a line there all along. That line was the threshold to their home that he'd never crossed. A boundary that gave him freedom and her a fishbowl of swirling anxiety.

She shifted on the hard wooden bench, sitting bones tired, lower back aching as she hunched deeper into the shape of a despondent 'O'. Because Jacky was more generic than she liked to admit. She wanted to be liked, loved, even. She was not dissimilar to other human beings in that. Only she wasn't so generic as to admit it. She straightened her back, creaking and crunching like eggshell. She opened another tab, made her selection, and picked up her phone.

She dreamed about him that night, and the doctor and the journalists. A crowd of yapping paparazzi dogs: Mark, their front man, taunting her with a larger-than-life cartoon camera that he pushed in her face, fingers tip-tapping the trigger button, its flashes frightening her. They pushed her until she fell, plummeting backwards into a cosmic swirl of sparkle and oily coloured-clouds. It went on until the lurching in her stomach woke her. She looked out through her glass wall, at the shadowy shrubs. She listened to the hooting of owls, fluttering of birds, fidgeting of squirrels, and she suddenly felt like some kind of deranged Snow White living in the woods with her entourage of forest friends. And it was Mark's fault. He'd made her feel this way.

21

Something about his mother calling made him crumble. It hadn't been a remarkable conversation. But it had come at the vulnerable time, while he was packing his bags in his Stockholm Airbnb. As he prepared to make his way back to London, back to the anxiety-riddled realities of his life.

They spoke once a week, he'd really had to limit the calls. He'd told her in the language of 'boundaries' he'd heard his classmates use. So arrogant, the way students are. Like he didn't need her. It was when he and Jacky had just started dating. Back then, he felt powerful. It stung now, remembering how good he'd made her feel. How needed. Life had been an easy dance. Floating between her and the rest of the cohort. This easy detachment that made everyone fall at his feet. Good times. His mother's whimpering voice down the line reminded him of that feeling. Of being in his strength, even with Jacky.

When did that change? Something had given, some invisible caving under pressure. He'd lost his perfect form, an easy strength that had made them so mutually reinforcing. In the language of his classmates, their interdependence had turned to co-dependency.

He looked around the room. Its simple white walls, its absence of design. Its Ikea furniture.

He missed feeling powerful.

He told his mum that. Her unconditional love had drawn the truth out of him. It always did. To be loved like that. He felt guilty now, for pushing her away. It was Jacky's talk about streamlining, about getting rid of emotional clutter. Completely psychopathic, he now realised. It was probably just all a way to claim him for herself. His poor mother had waited patiently for him to come to his senses. She'd just accepted it, given him his space. This woman, married into the most conventional of relationships, knew about healthy boundaries.

The joke was that even as Jacky had tried everything in her power to control him, he knew it was Clarissa she really wanted. He knew love, the kind his mum had shown him, when he saw it. At some level, when Clarissa came into the picture, he knew he was done for. Maybe it had triggered in him an unconscious but very healthy self-protective mechanism. He must have learnt it from childhood. Clarissa was what Jacky wanted, and maybe even what she needed. There was some kind of equanimity between them, he could tell. Something less functional.

They were equals in a way him and Jacky never were. He'd learnt what love was, Jacky never had. But Clarissa was showing her. In ways that he couldn't. He'd watched her learn, slowly, what it was to have someone there unconditionally. Eventually, he knew, something would happen to make her understand the utter importance of that. He'd sensed how their inevitable ending would be Jacky's beginning. He'd braced himself, but he'd broken all the same. He'd been so alone.

Mummy. Maybe the first woman in his life had ruined him. She'd always let him be so free. She'd let him exist without demanding reciprocity, without confronting him with the impact of his actions on her. Never setting curfews, imposing chores, never a single reprimand. Just unending affection. Entirely boundary-*less*. She'd made him feel safe, *too* safe. He didn't understand the risk of relationships, the possibility of devastation. Jacky's visions had made sense to him because free and open was how he had always understood a bond. But that secure upbringing had exposed him to abuse. He'd never expected a woman to hurt him.

He didn't know what to do with it. All that pain. So he told his mum. She said that she had always thought that Jacky was *a cold, insect-like woman*. Somehow that didn't help. It gave him no answers. He was debilitated by his mother's condition-less embrace. He had nowhere else to go from that infinitely-loving place. It was just too good.

And now, he would never venture out again.

Mark ended the call. He brushed aside the neatly stacked shirts and white and black t-shirts he'd arranged on the bed; they were from a time, all of fifteen minutes ago, when he'd still had the strength to order his feelings through menial tasks. Now, he just wanted to die. He crawled into the clearing and curled up into a ball, phone cradled in the palm of his hand and held to his heart, so that it would continue to speak, to give him the answers. *Melodramatic*, Jacky would say, *hyperemotional*, or, the real killer: *pathetic*. But he didn't care. He was sad. He tucked his head deeper into the void at the centre of his foetal position, and let his tears soak the off-the-shelf, DVALA sheets.

22

Steam poured like dragon's breath from a vat of liquid nitrogen. Jacky had instructed them to give her a tour of the lab. That had been her condition, if they wanted her custom. She wanted to see where her eggs would end up. They were very accommodating. A young company, eager to prove themselves. She appreciated that sort of unmoderated dedication.

'We've frozen eggs for some big names. It's all confidential, but just to say, rest assured, we specialise in guarding the genes of our society's *crème-de-la-crème*. Cream eggs! Your eggs will feel right at home.'

She took in the young woman leading her around the lab – hair pulled tightly back, a clean, round disc of a face. Young. The girl had been told to flatter the client, and she did it without resentment. While that seemed pathological to Jacky, the subservience suited her well. This was all part of the service at Elite Eggs. The name, Jacky thought, evoked a Noah's Arc scenario. Of humanity, faced with apocalypse, loading a spaceship with the DNA they wanted to replicate. It occurred to Jacky that she didn't know anyone whose genes she thought really warranted another run at life. Which proved she wasn't really a eugenicist.

They'd dressed Jacky in scrubs, a mask over her face, gloves coating her fingers, the plastic growing sweaty despite the liquid frost tumbling from the vats. She looked around at the lines of gleaming microscopes, a few occupied by concentrated scientists staring deep into their specimens. Her tour guide watched her watch them.

'They're removing unnecessary cells before they transfer them to fresh petri dishes.'

Jacky liked the idea that you could strip a potential life down to the bare essentials. Really, that's what most people wanted, just without the renunciation it entailed. But efficiency was a hard-earned commodity. It was a privilege to trim the fat. Wrapped in clammy plastic, Jacky felt suddenly calm, so reaffirmed in her life's work. Reassured that everyone wanted what she had. The apex of society's ambitions had to be the image of the lonely astronaut, a person floating around space in their own private suit. People were too afraid to take that leap, worried they'd change their minds and want to turn back, back to an overcrowded planet with plenty of people to blame for their dissatisfaction. Jacky remembered what she'd done it all for. That word Mark used but never understood: freedom.

Jacky watched the scientists a while longer. She wondered what they saw. Was it just a chore to them, like surgery, using their metal toothpicks to pick at life? Did they feel connected to the potential life forms? Inspired? Powerful? The tour guide pointed to a screen that showed her what they were doing. A bright pink plasma lit from behind, punctuated by cloudy grey and black dots like flies floating in syrup on a summer's day. Jacky thought of the dough of existence. How once you knew you could stretch it out so thin that holes appeared, there was really no going back. Once you knew that life was mutable, you'd forever wonder what to do with it.

Jacky watched the cells twitch as the scientists' pipettes moved them in the warm-tinted jelly. She watched the spaces between the cells, shifting blotches of negative light. It made her think of that chapel she'd visited with Mark, in the beginning. Like the microscopes and the cells, it had looked extra-terrestrial, the way it stood like a monolith in a remote German field. It had been cast around the frame of a hundred tree trunks. When the trunks were burnt away, it left a charred cavity, an oculus that, when lit by natural light, had the texture of roughened bark. When you stood at its base, surrounded beyond the walls of the chapel, by the relatives of the charred ancestral mould, it was like looking through nature's windpipe. Wide and open, endless breath, flowing through the scar of a human devastation. Life just flowing on. It took your breath away.

Jacky filled out the necessary forms and scheduled her first appointment. She had been convinced that her eggs had to be moved around with scientific tools, should be lowered into a plunging vat of liquid nitrogen, should travel in unchartered territory.

23

The grieving mother had come in to see her that day. There is no term like 'widow' for a mother who has lost her child, Clarissa thought as the ghost of a woman drifted in. There was something uniquely stunting about this form of loss. A backwards form of grief. None of the surrender to despair of most losses. This woman wasn't hankering for the warmth of lost memories, but for a whole life she had tried to give. There was no ending to that story, only the hollow aborted future that she had been left to live.

The woman had come to see her every week since the tragedy. It had been months now, and she was still stumped. Clarissa didn't know what to do. She thought that perhaps the situation required emergency interventions. That she had to focus quite intently on finding the woman something to live for. But her clumsy attempts felt premature and insensitive. She'd decided just to sit with her, as best as she could. To join her in her void. It reminded Clarissa of the struggle with Jacky. That draw to save her, knowing that Jacky had to save herself. That blurry distinction between supporting and saving she'd never quite understood. Despite her years of sitting with people, she was still tempted to do the heavy lifting herself. She wanted to *feel* the effort she was making. The strain of her muscles drawing in the thick waxy rope she used to sturdy her boat. She wanted to hear the creaking of wood in the act of holding against the ocean's might. She needed that reassurance to know she was trying.

Maybe the woman needed to feel her own strength, she thought.

'Can you tell me about him today?'

It was painful to ask her. But Clarissa would keep asking her. To suggest to the woman her unfathomable potential.

The woman didn't look at Clarissa. She was not interested in the world or its people, her senses were preoccupied with searching another place.

Clarissa knew she would have to repeat herself until the words reached her, wherever she was.

'Can you tell me what you remember about him from that day?'

The woman remained silent, her body a knot that refused to ease. Clarissa breathed through a flare of panic, aware of the damage she could do to a wound so open.

They sat in silence for a long time before the woman showed any sign of life. Her clasped hands moved, her fingers unclenched a little, allowing blood to flow to their blue-tinted tips. Clarissa watched the movement. They watched it together. That was all they did that day.

Clarissa made her way to the dockyard after work. It was 4pm on the brink of winter, so she knew she only had a few hours of daylight. But she needed something to soothe the dread she'd felt after seeing the mother. She needed the resistance of wood as she sanded it down, the smoothening under the caress of a brush. And she needed the punch of varnish to the point where her nasal cavity connected to her tear ducts. While she worked, she thought about life and how it only exists in relation to death. How the more life you create the more death you'll experience. She thought about the risks of all that love, and she felt a painful swell in her abdomen in anticipation of all the loss to come. All the hardening. As she forced the weight of her body into the sander she wondered if she would grow calloused and rough like the man she'd bought the boat from. Would she continue to turn to resistance to survive travesty?

Would she always need these metaphors of resistance to cope? Was strength the only way?

The boat always gave her what she needed. The comfort of a chill masked by the heating of her muscles, giving way to exhaustion that made her needs indisputable.

She thought about Jacky and the pain of loving her. About the way she belittled her to make herself feel strong. She laughed. A woman had lost a child and she was still thinking about Jacky. Every loss took her back to Jacky. That was why she took the risk of losing her.

24

Jacky was at home when the clinic called outlining the first course of hormone therapy that would be required to prepare her eggs for harvest. She'd spent the days since her visit to the clinic at home, flitting between the dead expanse of her inbox, Twitter and the papers her lawyers had sent over on her request. She had been investigating the procedures involved in renaming the company, but had been slowed down by the oppressive weight of Mark's radio silence across all telecommunications. No response to her provocation. Whether it had been serious or not, she wasn't sure. But the longer the silence lasted, the more resolute she became that she would forge ahead as Beetle Inc, and claim their legacy as her own.

The call from the clinic was a welcome distraction.

'Which makes these fertility hormones the equivalent to ploughing?' She was being sarcastic but the voice on the other end of the phone, a new voice she hadn't heard from before, answered sincerely:

'You could see it that way. We want to make sure we enrich your soil with all the right nutrients.'

The whole process sounded more agricultural than she

had envisioned. Gone were the promises of disembodied scientific precision. This was much too crassly mechanical.

'Now you understand the side effects, I suppose. You'll have to be prepared for some discomfort.'

Discomfort was the medical word for pain. That slippage was familiar to Jacky, who lived with many discomforts – aching back, grinding joints, glaring migraines – that over the years had escalated, along with the numerous pains that she had convinced herself were mere discomforts in the service of ambition. She was fully capable of deluding herself that she could keep pain at bay. But, while in the research stage of her existential egg journey, she'd shrugged the treatment's side-effects off as abstract potentialities, now the image of her blue and bloated body surfaced more ominously.

She hung up the phone and let her arm fall by her side. She stood, listless, in the centre of the living room. It was interesting, she'd never been so thrown off by the prospect of physical mutilation before. She'd never thought about it over the course of her training. It also occurred to her, however, that it had never been presented to her as an option in the past. At architecture school it had been more than a rite of passage, but an ongoing necessity. The difference, of course, was that the value of architecture was indisputable. The value of egg harvesting was not. She was more certain than ever, given the brutalisation that even the most scientifically rein-vention involved, that reproduction was very much optional.

It was a relief, at first, as she ended the call, knowing, at some level, that she had drawn a line under this. A form of closure just as the day was turning to night. She knew she wouldn't call them again, and she knew that she wouldn't answer their calls again. She hadn't exactly decided to discontinue treatment, but she had, from that moment, given herself permission to turn from it, to redirect herself, and accelerate in a different direction.

Only, suddenly, that didn't seem possible. As she stood there in the silent aftermath of the call, she found herself incapable of intention. She didn't know where to look. She wasn't paralysed, exactly, but her will had somehow disassociated from the network of vessels and tendons and limbs she had always known to be her body. She wasn't in pain, but it was difficult to know what she felt, her attention hovering solely in the soft space between her clavicles. She was aware of those two bones as nodes in her body's scaffolding, but only conceptually. What she felt was what she could only describe as a cool glow. She looked down at that space just above her chest and found the source of the unprecedented sensation. A perfect disc of moonlight lit up her skin so neatly, it looked like a piece of jewellery. Jacky raised her hand and placed it on the silver amulet, then followed the light beam to its source with her eyes. She followed it through the glass, wet and liquid in the blue light, out and up to that big, cold orifice. She followed the beam back to her own body, down the beam like the spotlight of a search party or a stage. To be hunted or to be seen. She didn't know the difference. The worst would be to mistake one for the other.

Maybe it was that sense that she didn't know anything that reminded her of her empty drawers awaiting specimens. The sense that her eggs and her business were both strung in limbo. The sense that the poles of her world had lost their charge. The poles imposing order, dividing sense from nonsense, reality from unreality, love from hate, Mark from Clarissa. That they were all falsely opposed repetitions of the same delusion. That the house she lived in was just an optical illusion in the light of an undifferentiated unknown.

Maybe it was that sense that she didn't know anything gave her the courage she needed to enter into the wild that terrified her. It was night, after all. Primetime for cock-chafers.

25

There was a spotlight on that night. The moon illuminated everything like a shrill, overpowered lightbulb. It cast every detail in high relief. Blades of grass, pixelated in their clarity, each as if cast against the backdrop of all the others, each of them competing for realness.

Jacky had left her glass prism armed with about ten funnel traps on strings; strange little yellow contraptions that looked like bottles wearing conical hats. The trap's mechanism brought Jacky some pleasure. It worked using a pheromone dispenser, which released a species-specific sex hormone that lured in specifically males into the trap. She enjoyed the idea of seducing mini-Marks to their structured and orderly afterlife.

She set out to distribute the traps around the garden and its surrounding parameters. While anger and nihilism had made her brave, she was still cautious. She held her phone outstretched, following the blue square of the screen's light, rather than the torch function, as it brought her some pleasure to see that the blue gleamed in a similar tone to the moon.

It looked hyper-real, the scene she'd been drawn into. She stumbled back in the face of it. Her earthly body couldn't handle it. It was just too perfect. Her heart raced the way it did after one too many espressos. She clutched her phone to her heart space, using it like an amulet to protect her from the moonlight's acid beam. She imagined her skin singed to frayed rags the colour of rust, remnants of fat and flesh drooping from singed bones. Holding her breath, she walked on.

She wandered further from the house than she'd ever been.

Tonight, she wanted more. The murmur of her heart propelled her on like a wind-up toy.

She reached a barbed wire fence that marked some kind of division. She'd never studied the surrounding territory on a map, not even while drawing up the designs; the space outside her vision hadn't interested her. She didn't know what lay beyond. Perhaps a farmer owned the land. It occurred to her that she'd feel safer inside the house knowing who her neighbour was. Now that she basically lived there alone. There had to be a human out there who, in topographical terms, was adjacent to her own existence. She wanted to shake the farmer's hand. She wanted to see his leathery face, the twinkle in a pair of kind eyes telling her simple truths about herself.

She checked the time on her phone. It was late, eleven at night, she'd been walking for a while. Much too late to drop by on anyone, but that urgent desire to meet the imaginary farmer drove Jacky on. It drove her to attempt to heave one of her legs up and over the barbed wire fence. She watched her leg go, it appeared to her that day as exceptionally spindly, the way it shot up like a sprig of grass from her heavy boot. She swung with all her might, aiming for the freshly-ploughed field that awaited her on the other side.

She didn't really believe she would make it. After years of physical inactivity, movement restricted to concentrated frowning and industrious hands, and minimal calorific intake, her muscles seemed to have prematurely atrophied at the dawn of her fourth decade. She had become a brittle and stick-like woman. Just a hunched posture atop two crooked wires. Despite her momentous effort, it was just barely enough to fling her leg up, so that it landed on the fence, barbs severing her thigh painfully in several places. The jolt of pain caused the other, still-grounded knee to fold, her weight pulling her down atop a spike with a meaty squelch.

Jacky cried out into the night. She heard her moan echo as if from afar. It was agony, but she didn't reach for her phone. She could have done it, she had the physical strength to call an ambulance, but she didn't want to. She just wanted to hang there.

She wanted to stop.

Hanging there like a limp sausage, she discovered new thoughts. Thoughts too dangerous to concede, connected to rest and stagnation. Like the thought that she wanted to be right more than she wanted the truth. That was why she let them take her words and stuff them down her oesophagus, into the body of an arrogant and unfeeling woman. Or that language of architecture was the best language she had but that it had failed her. That she had only managed to trap herself in trying to be anything completely. That her buildings were lies. That what she said in the interviews were lies. That everything that happened in the space between her reality and theirs, was a lie. That was the worm burrowing itself through tissue and bone into the wound of her leg. The truth was, that the vertigo that frayed tunnel of flesh gave her, was better than anything architecture had ever made her feel.

It wasn't the optimal time to be discovering the appeal of immobility. Just as she might be going it alone. She felt an electric surge down her spine, threatening seizure. What would become of her if she surrendered to that tantalising possibility?

She craned her neck to look at the stars. That mysterious splay of atoms she'd barely bothered with since university. They were the glimmers on the periphery of her streamlined vision. She noticed a pair of swirls resembling the eyes of an anime sumo wrestler from one of the comics Mark used to read as a student, before they'd streamlined leisure time out of his life. She imagined linking arms with the wrestler, his turkey wings pressing into her. She wanted to cling to that feeling of substance, to let him carry her with him through the holes of his eyes into an abundant universe.

She let her head fall back down. Near-to delirious, now, her tongue limply hung from her mouth, her bug-eye specs dangling from her crooked head. She hung there, mangled and deformed, and at the same time, as her eyes bulged, reaching out for more. Ecstatic.

26

Jacky opened her eyes. The moon had moved, she must have lost consciousness. Perhaps the rustling had woken her. She flopped her head up and down, still limp like a scarecrow.

When she finally managed to heave it up, she found herself eye-to-eye with a fox. She'd only ever seen foxes from the inside of her car, usually as road kill. She looked into its eyes as her consciousness ebbed and flowed. Dark, oily beads receding to somewhere otherworldly, like the night sky.

She was the closest to truth she'd ever been and it was also a performance.

She was so used to them all watching. To people judging her in life, in work, now through the glass of her house. She was so used to it that she'd internalised their stares. She lived as if they were always there. She'd forgotten what it was to live without them. Without their witnessing, she wasn't sure if she'd believe she existed at all.

The truth was, that she wanted to look like someone who needed saving. *How do you like me now?* She wanted her body to say to the world. *This is Jacky MacKenzie when she stops fighting. This is her when she stops being a bitch.*

She stared into the fox's eyes. A picture began to build around them. A long, protruding snout, deeper auburn giving way to paler shades of fluff, pointed ears recapitulating the same elegance of its body and tail. She let the fox witness her.

They'd once agreed that Mark had canine appeal. It came to her then, in her semi-conscious state, one of the more tender episodes of their streamlined romance. It was in the early days, long before the unsympathetic journalist had coined that sticky dub, but, in that moment, she remembered, how others had used it too. Her classmates had landed on the same coleopteran analogue for her inhumanity. They had named her long before the journalist. Neither she, nor Mark had been surprised when the journalist repeated it all those years later. It had appeared to them as predictable, almost inevitable, because they'd been bracing themselves for it all along.

Back then, Jacky had turned to Mark, and told him how hurt she was that she had been compared to a creature so cold, and worse, with its PVC shine, tacky.

She wrote to him at the time, which they did to overcome Jacky's disgust reflex when it came to vulnerability. He told her to write her feelings down, so she'd feel less exposed. And so, she did.

Dear Mark,

They're calling me 'The Beetle' now. I'm embarrassed that I care.

The words materialised before her now, as if scrawled on papyrus. The artefact had lurked in her subconscious for a while. She'd never dared to look at it.

She remembered now, how Mark had responded, in that language they shared, full of symbols and certainty.

Jacky,

It's an ode to streamlining, don't you see? For the Ancient Egyptians, those pioneering architects, the scarab was an incarnation of the sun god, Khepri. Its hieroglyph referred variously to the ideas of existence, manifestation, development, growth and effectiveness. I couldn't have chosen you a better symbol myself. Throughout the periods of Egyptian history, the scarab was used for amulets. It was a symbol for rebirth after death, placed in the cavity of the heart space of mummified bodies. Don't you see how you're iconic? You just have a scarab where the heart should be.

That was the kind of romance they allowed themselves in the beginning.

Mark,

You have this way of turning weakness into strength. You do the same with our buildings – you find the weakest structural points and you make them the centre piece. It's that sense of compassion that I've always admired in you. But our shared body can't have two hearts, so I'm calling you Anubis. Anubis is a compilation of jackal, dog and fox. Sometimes a black canine with pointed ears, others a muscular man with the head of a canine. Anubis is the god of the afterlife. The Egyptians assigned this animal to protect them from the threat he symbolised. You see? That same ingenious conversion.

Anubis and Khepri. Soon we'll be immortal.

Jacky heard those words clearly now. This subliminal message telling her that she'd dug her own grave. How she'd assigned him the role of overlord. How she'd made him her only source of strength. Jacky realised now, that it had all been prophesied. That microscopic patterns had determined the colour of her skin. *The principle of iridescence.* That her current situation had been created by the pattern of her choice, repeated through time, to be seen even if it meant being hunted. And so perhaps it wasn't even her classmates who had named her, really, but she who had named herself, before it was a conscious choice, let alone a word.

All along, they had known. Jacky had always known that eventually a bigger pool of critics would discover her true nature. She had lived with the simmering knowledge of her beetle-like ways, had anticipated imminent exposure and it had animated her. It was the source of her acceleration. And Mark had banked on it. The overlord had counted on their venture coming to a clean and definitive end. She couldn't blame him, they'd both agreed. This was the truth of the house they'd built.

27

Like beetles, meat can be iridescent too. Certain cuts show the same structural colouration, based on microscopic refractions and reflections. If people abandoned their prejudices and approached meat as they did architecture, they'd find it had the same beauty as a prism.

And it makes sense, that the muscular fibres once charged with kinetic potential beam luminescent. We have to surrender to experience our microscopic destiny.

Jacky looked down at the patch on her leg, still covered by a surgical plaster. She pulled the sticky peel back, and leaned in closer, fascinated by the ooze of antiseptic mixed with her body's goo. A scab was starting to form around the edges. It resembled a landmass emerging from the ocean. She imagined getting on Clarissa's boat, setting out to find an island like that. What supplies would she have gathered if she'd planned for her present isolation? Who would she have chosen to share isolation with? Clarissa or Mark? Or neither. Maybe she'd have chosen neither.

She stared blankly at the nurses and doctors who passed by her bed, redressing her wound, intermittently asking her questions about 'suicidal thoughts' and babbling inanely about nothing much at all. Jacky didn't have the energy for this kind of extra-terrestrial communication.

She felt stranger than ever. Despondent, still, as the vague memory of semi-lucid insights lingered in her weary, partially sedated brain. But her body felt calm. As if she'd thrown herself off some ledge, expecting to plummet to her death, only to find that she had lived. An innate confidence she'd found, that her body had found, in the face of endings she thought she couldn't survive.

'Maybe we can talk about what you would need to keep going for now.'

Some young person was talking to her, perhaps a kind of mental health worker or something equally paradoxical. Apparently, they'd been in conversation for a while, because his question implied she'd answered previous questions. Saying that, people made assumptions about her all the time.

'That won't be necessary.'

The boy nodded. He looked upset.

'You're going to have to toughen up if this is your chosen line of work.'

The boy smiled self-consciously. Jacky didn't reciprocate.

'Let me save you some time. Survival is the least of my worries.'

The boy cleared his throat.

'That's what worries me, Ms MacKenzie. You've told me that you're experiencing suicidal ideation. So it's my job to help you figure out a plan to keep you safe.'

'And I'm telling you, that's not my priority.'

Jacky looked at the boy with disdain. She swore she could see him tearing up again, so she turned to her side and waited for him to leave.

As she lay there, recovering from the onslaught of patron-
ising people, she thought about the nature of her injury. She
was lying there, with a respectable scar trailing the length
of her thigh, only they'd hidden it with bandages. Nurses
treating her like she'd transgressed. It was funny, she thought,
as she lay in that liminal twilight of the hospital ward, how
context changed everything. How they'd celebrated her
physical commitment in one place, then berated her for it in
another. Professors and colleagues venerating her saint-like
asceticism; hospital staff treating her like a petulant child.
How one moment critics lauded her designs as progressive,
the next fascist. She thought about how powerful, whole and
full she was at work, and how withered and inadequate she
became in the spaces in between. She looked down at her
bandaged leg and wondered how it was that she only felt
pathological in her time off work.

That night, she dreamed of sparkling, rainbow-coloured
hunks of meat, all lined up on a butcher's counter like the
angel cake her mother used to reluctantly feed family guests
on birthdays. She dreamed, and remembered how, as a
child, she'd inspected the food colouring and thought of the
planet's layers. How she'd bitten into it imagining she could
bite cross sections out of the Earth. She dreamed of her
dismembered teeth floating towards the radioactive treat,
incisors clicking as her teeth chomped thin air.

When she woke, she knew it was time to go. It made
sense, that with the excavations on the fence, she'd unin-
tentionally dug up thoughts that came dangerously close to
resembling childhood memories. Pointless, uninformative.
They shocked her into awareness. She'd slowed down to a

debilitating pace. She propped herself up against the flat and itchy hospital cushions and turned her attention to the UV drip in her arm. She conjured the image of the shiny sparkles of a butcher's finest cut, and ripped the needle out of her pale and sickly arm. She picked up her glasses from her bedside tray, snatched a bandage from a trolley on the way out, which she wrapped calmly around her wound to stymy the fountain of blood, as she hobbled to the exit in her surgical gown.

28

The woman had spoken that day. Clarissa was beyond relieved. It was one of those milestone moments in a therapist's career. She'd been reaffirmed in her carefully honed instincts. Reassured that she had the necessary toolkit to help, not hurt, people.

Not that it was at all about her, but she'd needed some sign of progress. She was failing miserably on other fronts. She hadn't heard from Jacky in weeks. She'd panicked for a few days, images of people disappearing in oceans fresh on her mind, but she'd put those thoughts to bed. She was always telling Jacky how her way of doing things wasn't sustainable. But she had to look at herself too. She couldn't be pandering to Jacky all the time. *Support, don't save*, she told herself. Jacky was not a child, definitely not *her* child. They had to break that unhealthy dynamic.

But it was difficult to silence the gnawing in her gut, that sense of personal failure at the state of their relationship. Part of her didn't believe that Jacky would ever really come to her. That the only way to draw affection out of Jacky, was to grab her and bite into her, to make her forget she needed you, to turn that need into desire. How long had it been? Five, seven years? Time had passed but they hadn't moved. It helped, in those moments, to remind herself how isolated she'd been prior to Jacky. That awkward tangentiality to women too full of something unfamiliar, something fleshy like the inside of a tropical fruit she didn't recognise. It had always made her want to scrape it out of them, to hollow them out so that they'd share her emptiness. It was easy to forget loneliness, since there was always more distracting her.

The days were getting darker. The kind of weather that did wonders for a relationship. Nights full of the cosy burrowing that brought you closer to someone. But for lone ships, it was a death sentence. Clarissa had chosen to stay home that afternoon, but didn't know what to do with herself. She stood, looking out the freshly painted window frame of her front room. In her forty years of moving between ocean and land, she'd done relatively well at protecting herself. She had painted, built and polished, she had made the structures of her life strong and bright. And still, it was difficult to resist the force of efflorescence, salt and water gnawing at the walls of her house. The dilapidation of a seaside town was not as charming up close, it turned out. Hollow but full with a cool breeze of rejection that made everything she did feel insubstantial.

The woman had spoken that day.

The first half of the session they'd sat together in their, by now, less uncomfortable, silence, watching the knot of her cold hands for signs of a future. That day, the pinkies had lifted, the movement passing visibly to her chest like a big, sad wave.

'We gave him that boat.'

The woman groaned, in the grip of a pain that threatened to strangle her. She closed her eyes.

'I had him on my lap. Had a big graze on his knee. Hair all straw-like, he never let us wash it. He still had his shorts on, t-shirt, we were going to change him for his swim.'

She choked, trying to take her first breath in a while.

'I had him on my lap and he was playing with that stupid boat. I mean, it was beautiful. His dad had made it for him. But we shouldn't have let him. And he was messing around with it, and I told him to put it away. And his skin smelled of sunscreen, that soft little person smell, you know?'

Clarissa watched her, working hard to contain her own moisture.

'Favourite towel, blow-up shark, armbands, snacks. Colouring stuff, books, boat. He kept telling us to bring his boat.'

She gasped for air now, the riverbed of her face flooding with tears.

'But maybe we pushed him to do it, you know, maybe he was fed up, all that fussing. Maybe he just wanted to get away. And play with his boat. Maybe we ruined it. But it wasn't really us, it was me. I was his mother. I should've known. I was his mother.'

Clarissa moved across the formal distance that separated them, then, and grabbed the mother's cold but free right hand, twining her own fingers through the gaps of the woman's knuckles, squeezing hard. She sat with the woman, besides her body rocking back and forth with relentless life.

A Scarab Where the Heart Should Be

Clarissa closed her eyes, letting the aftershocks of the woman's grief pass through her, processing, the way she had learned she had to, to survive. She trusted the process. She just needed reminding sometimes. She knew there was no escaping the weather. That is why she had chosen to live there, a place that had appeared to her whimsically honest, with its storybook houses whose stories had turned them to sand.

29

Jacky burst through the door in a cold sweat. She realised, as she entered the house and caught her reflection in one of the glass walls, that her surgical gown gaped at the back, and so the taxi driver and whoever else had watched her make her way from the hospital entrance to the car, had been exposed to a view of her shrivelled posterior. Nothing new there, she thought. She was intimately familiar with the experience of feeling exposed.

She stood still for a while, panting in the hall. She moved her gaze between the glass sheaths, soothed by the slices of light and neat lines. She looked up, through the glass ceiling, to the floor above. It didn't take long to confirm that he wasn't home. Another one of the advantages of clear glass.

No one had visited her in the hospital. No one had bothered to check in with her after days of radio silence. If it had all been a test, it had told her all she needed to know. *Alone, alone, alone*, she murmured in a singsong, fluttering her arms like beetle wings. And that reminded her to check the traps.

A Scarab Where the Heart Should Be

They were overflowing. She was euphoric. A treasure trove of big, beetle jewels heaped like bundles of grapes. She emptied one of the traps on her workbench and set to work.

Rosemary Beetle
Chrysolina americana
6-8mm

Beautiful.

                           exotic adventurers.

metallic green and purple stripes.

Swollen-thighed beetle
Oedemera nobilis
6-11mm

excellent pollinators,

            integrally stylish.

Rainbow leaf beetle
Chrysolina cerealis
5.5-10mm

        ...memories of flight.

Jacky worked her way through the haul, cataloguing descriptions, trying to stay objective. Once documented, she pinned the bugs down inside the drawers in tidy rows. It was incredibly satisfying. The process was deeply creative and reassuringly familiar. Ordering the information that struck her as most significant. That same metamorphosis that turned nature into architecture.

Rose Chafer
Cetonia aurata
20mm

Iridescence: a beautiful shield.

Jacky let the facts glide over her like water off a beetle's back.

Lesser stag beetle
Dorcus parallelipipedus
30mm

All of them had chosen...

She catalogued her way through the heap of beetles, filling her drawers with the silent kin. In each of them was an answer. Each had developed a possible way to be. Every species had found a focus for this finite life, and with it, a distinct hypothesis about the point of it all.

Deathwatch beetle
Xestobium rufovillosum
5-9mm

a form of haunting.

As she pinned them down, the carpet of jewels revealed a new truth to her. She'd always imagined legacy as the answer, but as she took in her intricate tapestry, she realised that she'd fallen privy to a severely limiting human adaptation. She'd been trapped in a linear history, one based on succession and offspring. That story was the product of vertical relations in space. But there were horizontal relations too. Time that moved outwards, not always, unimaginatively on. There was a way of living amongst her beetle kin. She didn't have to move forward in time to reach them. She just had to sit back and let her own interconnectedness reveal itself to her. She could be part of this world without exerting her influence over it. Without trying to contain it or decide what it all meant. The beetles were showing her how.

The beetles were closing in on her.

Jacky sat amongst her collection, legs spread apart, back hunched over the intricate work, the crosshatch of her hospital gown just another exoskeleton, in a constellation of species. She worked away, still weak from blood loss, until the drawers were full. She stacked the drawers inside the cabinet and took in her beetles. As a collective, they were rich and dynamic in death. She opened the drawers in succession. Top, middle, bottom then top again. Opening, closing, reopening. Her pace quickened. Their modular bodies formed patterns with her movement, fuelling her urge to multiply. She stopped. She needed a mirror. Her eyes fixed on the one hanging in the next-door bedroom. Somehow, she lifted herself off the ground, floating towards the closet, carried by an evolutionary pull, stronger than her stitched-up limbs. She unlodged the bar on which her beetle-clothes hung, and charged, without a moment's hesitation, at the mirror on the wall. Shards of light fell to the ground. She collected the biggest fragments and carried them back to her work room. She held up the various pieces to the top drawer of beetles, catching their colour, watching patterns bounce in bursts from the mirror onto the glass walls and back again. She left the pieces there at the perfect angle, and got up, twirling in the taxonomic kaleidoscope she'd created. She laughed, euphoric. Repetitions lifting her to flamboyant flight, as she joined the blazing exodus, moving with beams turning to waves. Up, not broken. Lifted, on the backs of the beetle's wings, out of the house, out of herself. She spun until she collapsed, shards of glass protruding from her torn and open skin.

Cockchafer
Melolontha melolontha
2.5-3cm

The beetles were closing in on her,

    unleashing doubts.

Words were dangerous eggs.

30

She tasted the dust. She couldn't believe it at first, but it was true; actual dust had gathered in the nook of the back of her knee. A silvery powder like metal shavings. How long had she been laying there, her legs at refracted angles, face turned up to the sky? For a moment, she was sure she could see the ghostly shadows of vultures circling overhead. They didn't know what glass was, she thought. Perhaps, if she'd lain there long enough, they'd have found out. Perhaps they would have turned their streamlined heads to the roof of her house, and been met, for the first time, with the hard resistance of a human defence.

Jacky considered whether or not to move. Her limbs were tingling from lack of blood flow, stinging in places, from the cuts to her skin. But part of her wanted to just be flesh with no consciousness.

Mark called then, rousing her from the brink of extinction. She turned to her side, brought face to face with a trail of beetles she had yet to categorise. She answered her phone without moving her eyes from a particularly fine exemplar of a *Cantharis rustica*.

'I wanted to talk to you,' he said, from some faraway place. 'I hope you don't resent me.'

'Why would I resent you, Mark?'

'Just with all the silliness going on, I thought maybe you'd expected me to come and see you.'

He was right. Jacky did resent him. She resented him for using the word silliness, like the constant attack at her being by hordes of strangers was nothing more than the playground jibes of school children.

'It's nothing I haven't dealt with before.'

'That's true.' He said quickly, almost grateful. 'And I suppose you have Clarissa.'

'What does that mean?'

'Just, I suppose you had her to talk to.'

Why weren't you there to talk to?

Jacky cleared her throat.

'I'm freezing my eggs.' She wasn't sure why she felt the urge to tell him after she'd decided not to go ahead. Some kind of future-proofing.

'How very progressive of you.'

'Says the man lauded for trialling the four-day work week.'

'I wanted to talk to you about that.' There was a pitchiness in his voice that made Jacky think he might tip into a state of emotion. But then he paused, suddenly distracted. 'You don't even want children.'

'That's not the point.'

Mark coughed. Jacky heard a muffled voice in the background. Light, feminine. Maybe she was imagining it.

'Where are you.'

He coughed again.

'Just at work.'

'Right. In your new office.'

'I think they got the wrong end of the stick.'

'We don't need to discuss it.'

'I just want you to know that I didn't mean to go behind your back.'

'So it is true.'

He cleared his throat, again.

'For god's sake Mark, out with it.'

'There's another firm, yes.'

'How long?'

'That's the thing I wanted to explain. It's not new. It's coming out now is so unfortunate. Makes it look like, I don't know—'

'Like a rat jumping ship as it's sinking. Is that how the expression goes?'

'That wasn't my intention.'

'It's very clever.'

It was worse than the journalists could have known. Jacky had realised it immediately. That if the rumours were true, it would never have been a reactionary escape. It would always have been a structural flaw.

'You always talked like this was it for you.'

'It was.'

'But you had this safety net all along? It cheapens the whole endeavour somewhat, don't you think?'

He paused. She pictured him there on the other end of the line, poised like a scrawny praying mantis, about to deliver the real stinger.

'You see, you're jealous. I always knew it. You always acted like you didn't care about exclusivity. But I knew you couldn't handle it, not really. That's why I hid it.'

Jacky wanted to ask him if there was someone else, too. If that was another truth he'd decided she couldn't handle, but she didn't want to detract from the real betrayal. So she said nothing, savouring the little power she still had to make him squirm.

'But now that it is out, I think it's a good time to talk about our future.'

'You mean our company's future?' She was pleading. It was there in the undercurrent of her voice, subtle but undeniable. Like the cockchafer's hum. She knew he could hear it too, and that he was choosing to ignore it. And while it left her her dignity, it proved his utter indifference.

'I think it's good this came out, because I think we've stopped talking about the future. We stopped checking in and that's how we've ended up going in different directions. It's just, you don't care about legacy, you know, you never have. Or maybe you do but... all this controversy. You can't force people to think your way. You have to go with the times.'

'I'm freezing my eggs. I'm all about the future now.' Jacky chuckled although she wanted to cry.

He sighed. 'You're laughing at me.'

'It's hard to talk when you're never here.' She really was pleading.

'I'll come and see you. Tomorrow. I'll be at the house early evening. We'll have a proper talk.'

She nodded like he could hear her.

'Jacky?'

'Yes.'

He hung up.

She dropped the phone limply to the ground and stared ahead of her, cheek still planted to the floor. She was relieved that he'd called ahead. She wasn't ashamed of her dishevelled appearance, floored amidst shards, and still in the blood-stained surgical gown with her arse on display. But she knew how people tended to demonise destruction. He wouldn't understand. Reluctantly, she reassembled her body. She dragged the disjointed levers of her elbows back to alignment, the bars of her legs back into their regular parallel. Her joints creaked like a tightening bench vice. She rubbed her sandpaper finger tips together, trying to restore the sensation of touch. She rubbed them across her joints, softening her body's edges into something less broken.

He arrived when he said he would. She watched him from her seat at the table as he entered the kitchen space. She didn't get up. She watched him as he looked for something to criticise. He purveyed the room, then pricked his ears, as if listening for the sound of crumbling. Jacky sat nervously, hyperaware of the chaos that loomed overhead, a shimmering avalanche that was visible, as everything was, through the glass ceiling overhead. As if he could read her thoughts, he looked up.

'What on earth have you been doing?'

She stared at him wide-eyed for a moment, then remembered her newfound autonomy, and shrugged.

'Inspiration.'

She watched the light bend in Mark's thick-framed lenses. In the early days he'd always worn thin, wire frames. Now he wore glasses with a more Scandinavian sensibility.

Acetate curved into the playful caricature of its original, the quirky seriousness that had become the signature style of creatives who succumbed to the allure of purchasable precedents – none of the risk, all of the status. It suited him, that performed minimalism.

He peered at her over the tops of his frames.

'You need to clear that up.'

'Yes.'

Their gazes locked in a silent showdown. Mark eventually sighed and turned to the espresso machine. He flicked switches and turned handles with a painful familiarity. They were just empty gestures now. He removed his glasses and rubbed his eyes while the espresso dripped and steamed. His eyes were tired, crow's feet had deepened since she last saw him, perhaps only a month ago. They made him look disconcertingly kind.

He carried two cups to the kitchen table and sat down on the chair at a right angle to her's. Once seated, he hesitated, then moved his chair in closer, metal scratching over the tiled floor. It wasn't something he wanted to do. She watched him wrestle with his posture in the space that demanded intimacy. He settled for a limp hand on her knee, an unfortunate choice as that happened to be the edge of the hump of bandages she had covered with the draping of a bug-like garment. This sparked further interrogations.

'What is that?'

He lifted the garment in a lapse of his newfound formality, to inspect the bundle underneath.

Jacky pulled the fabric from his hand, wrapping it around her leg protectively.

'Don't.'

He looked at her, now, with a sadness that remained disingenuous.

'Are you okay?'

'It's fine.'

His eyes moved between her face and leg. 'Did you do that?'

Jacky shot up.

'Why does everyone think I'm a loose cannon.'

Mark leaned forward, resting his chin pensively on his fist, as if she'd presented him with a problem he had to solve.

Jacky watched him angrily for a while, then dropped back down, deflated, to her seat of Scandinavian redwood. Mark's finger curled around his espresso cup's handle. He took a sip.

'I'm sorry I've been so absent. You know I respect you. That's one thing that's never changed.'

Respect. It was a word that had crept into their conversations over the years. It hadn't been there at first. Decisions made based on 'respect'. Tasks shuffled this way or that, truths withheld, promises broken, but all out of 'respect'. That word had begun to displace all others. The more respect there was, it seemed, the less need for anything else. Affection, trust, companionship, all annihilated by that bogus word he'd picked up somewhere new-agey and vacuous.

'If you mean we've always understood each other, I used to think that was true.'

'It was. It was out of respect that I took some space. I mean, that's what we always said, right?'

'There's a difference between space and distance.'

He diverted his gaze to the table and took the last swig of his espresso.

'I worked for us just like you did, you can't say I wasn't there. I was always determined to, despite—' He put his cup down. 'It was a kind of ruthlessness I admired in you, Jacky. It was honestly awesome. Sometimes it scared me. Your focus. I had it too but yours was sort of bloodthirsty. It was like you wanted to destroy everything first, like you were clearing the ground to build something just for you. And you even seemed to enjoy it.'

'Ok so I've got a bit of anti-institutional flair. But you knew I had my insecurities. I was just thinking, the other day—'

She stopped herself. She wasn't going to give him the satisfaction of getting sentimental.

'I learned to suppress my doubts because they didn't help us. We both did. We didn't entertain them. It's like you don't remember. Failure wasn't an option. You were in the room with me Mark. We did it together. I fought hard, you fought hard. And we guarded ourselves. And it's good that I did, with the hostility you've exposed me to.'

He looked out over the garden, trying to look all meditative.

'Look, Jacky. We always made sense. That's why I've been so determined. Just recently, it's been hard to relate to you. All those ideas we had, they came from a shared feeling, you know. These days you're just sort of cold.'

Cold. That icy tentacle of a word. It struck her in the raw and gaping wound he'd made of her.

'Do you see what I mean?' He took her hand now, squeezing it for the first time in years.

Jacky must have phased out, missed some crucial element of an explanation, because she hadn't heard one, nor did she understand what there was to explain. All she heard was an accusation, a low blow, an attack that confirmed his allegiance with everyone else.

'I don't want the gap between us to widen. I want to preserve the parts that will always make sense,' he said, with tears in his eyes that were entirely inexplicable.

31

Jacky was enjoying a workflow unlike anything she'd experienced since her early undergraduate days. Back then, when she'd first discovered the joy of conjuring. Her hands twisted and bent pieces of paper, miming the movements of Mark's young hands folding shapes in Soho. She felt loose, unrestrained by ideas about herself. Her heart raced as if up against some invisible timer, lurching hurriedly forward, reaching for the finish line, desperate for the certainty of that definitive moment.

Something had inspired her, she wasn't sure what. It must have been a microscopic patterning, something priming her for this creative leap. She'd designed a new kind of building.

It was inevitable, she realised, because art recapitulates life and her entire outlook had changed. Until now, architecture had just been a tool she'd used to frame and constrain the unknown, to assuage her unease, the way most architects did. Deeply self-centred. She was different now, her night on the fence had changed her. She had found a way to turn her buildings into vessels for exploration, not stagnation. Defying distinctions between life and death, beginning and ending, nature and civilisation. Her new designs would be the frames for unbound imagination.

They'd be coated in skin. She was going to make living, breathing, pulsating skin. She'd strap it across a mutable framework, allowing it to shapeshift like an evolving beetle. The whole thing would be charged, like a heart, pulsating with illusory life. She would patent the skin-like material: BeetleSkin.

She already knew how to make it. She'd made a gooey film using chloroform during her undergraduate once. She remembered being intrigued by it, although she'd only meant to use it as glue. It had dried into an elastic film, resistant but forgiving. It stretched like skin, growing thin and translucent, stretchmarks creeping like veins across its surface. At the time, she'd put the distracting sense of awe down to the fumes of the chloroform. Toxic was an understatement. There were no safety regulations, no masks or fume cupboards, as was characteristic of a department that gave Jacky creative freedom.

She would have to go to the office to make the skin. She never went there, it being a festering hub of distractions she could easily avoid. Designing could be done in solitude from home. The proof was in the pudding: she was efficient beyond belief. The only time her smooth workflow met any resistance was during the occasional meetings with juniors. The predictable millennial arrogance distilled into comments on 'outdated modes of dictatorial leadership', telling her that her 'absent genius act' was 'so passé'. Respect seemed to miss her in the appropriate places. She'd bled for her superiors. Their comments became further incentive to avoid her 'co-workers', which is what they now called employees.

She packed a bag, quickly, and plucked a long-line black blazer from the cupboard that she layered on top of the tailored trousers and button-up dress shirt she already had on. A pair of pointed patent leather brogues, dark-tinted bug-eyes, a flask of coffee and she was ready to go.

She arrived at the office at 6am. It was Monday morning. She hadn't slept. This, she knew, was the perfect precipice from which to throw herself into full-fledged creativity. She ignored the receptionist as she entered the building and hobbled, still sore in her injured leg, down the gleaming hallways, scanning her card at the various security code-guarded doors on the way, to the studio at the back of the building. She swung the door open and took in the industrial space. It was empty. She sighed with relief, dropped her bag on the nearest work bench and made her way to the storage cupboards to dig up the necessary materials.

Jacky had learnt a thing or two about how living beetles fly. This was her optimal frequency. Buzzing and wired and alone, her entire being had risen to her head, where it stayed now, condensed and barely breathing. A form of cerebral contortion that made her luxuriously oblivious to pain. She knew it was a volatile state of existence. The effects of Mark's harsh words simmered somewhere downstairs, turning her body gangrene, threatening with each bubble of stench to burst through the ceiling into awareness.

Perhaps those subliminal toxins had thrown her off. At first, the skin didn't come out the way Jacky knew it should. She'd used the same materials, the same method, but the result was unrecognisable, just turned to gloop.

She was tired now. The kind of tired that puts you in a state of undoing. Her skin tingled, threatening to evaporate from her spent frame. She conjured the memories of her chloroform-fuelled undergraduate days, recalling the process to ensure she hadn't missed any steps. It occurred to her that she must have been high on the gas for much of her studies. It had, unwittingly, been her drug of choice. In contrast to the stimulants her classmates preferred, she'd taken a sedative instead. She'd chosen a drug that was used as an early surgical anaesthetic. One famously used by military doctors during the American Civil War to perform amputations. A drug for the ruthlessness of amputation.

The memory of the fumes revived her confidence. It would be a building of pure possibility. Yes, it wouldn't just be the outside, but the inside too, that would look like human flesh. Inhabitants would lose all sense of where their body ended and the building began. They'd be connected, fully connected, to the structure of artificial flesh. It would be a place of vulnerable presence. Jacky had always tried to claim that space ironically, hiding in plain sight. She'd thought of it as defiance, but it had only been defensive. She'd fortified herself out of fear. She could admit that to herself now. And she could admit that she wanted more. She wanted to take the risk of connection. To close the distance between herself and the world. She would choose skin over glass.

It was imperative that the living building was born.

PART 3

AFTER
MEANING

PART 2

AFTER

MEANING

32

She hadn't heard him say it was over. He had said it, loud and clear, but she hadn't heard him. Maybe that was because in his lengthy speech about their incompatibilities, she'd been distracted by one particular point, subsidiary to the central thesis in his regard, but to her, the crux of it all. For in mentioning in passing the way she had neglected him, he'd confirmed a fear she had long held about herself – that she was, indeed, in line with popular opinion, a heartless bitch. That she didn't know how to love anyone, and that no one really loved her. An ungenerous and rather hasty inference, perhaps, but nothing that hadn't already been said about her, or that she hadn't, in her most self-loathing moments, already thought about herself.

She wasn't sure exactly why, but she knew that she hadn't heard him. This, in turn, meant that when the conversation ended and they parted ways, the conciliatory peck on her cheek that he gave her was no different from the thousands that had come before. She paid little attention to his departure as he walked out the glass door of the sleek, modernist masterpiece they had called home before they'd even lived there. She didn't even watch him, although she could have, through the glass walls, as he made his way to his Tesla and disappeared down their driveway and down a country road. She thought she'd be seeing him again soon – in that same lukewarm capacity that had become the default of their relationship. She thought that they'd continue the way they had been. For better or for worse.

This explains, of course, how following the end of that defining relationship, Jacky was able to return to work, seemingly entirely unaffected.

That, the many loyal critics who reported on the divorce would argue, was nothing new. She was, after all, rather heartless. Whether she'd heard him or not, they noted the speed with which she'd thrown herself into her next project. A desperate effort, they argued, to consolidate profits in anticipation of the financial hit that would come with their company's dismantling. Whatever the specifics, though, the facts were there: The Beetle didn't seem to notice, or didn't seem to care, that her husband had left her.

'It's her own fault!', the critics wrote. She had chosen this life of isolation. She had chosen to push everyone away. And, of course, Jacky would agree with them. She had quite deliberately developed the capacity to dismiss her feelings – all that loneliness and loss – as phantom pains. She had developed that strategy to suppress the inkling stirring in her. That the deliberate fissures in her relationship were just gaping expanses. Nothing more, and nothing less.

The feelings of utter desolation that overcame Jacky were by design, but that didn't make them deliberate. Jacky's artificial structure of a relationship was a feat of architecture, the closest any two people had ever come to an ideal. That didn't stop her soul from splitting as it tried to span the empty spaces her buildings contained. She hadn't heard him say it was over. She wasn't designed for this.

33

Jacky had turned a corner as a human and a leader. The skin was finally coming together. It now held as it stretched into plasma membranes that could span a frame. Jacky had challenged herself to produce ever-larger sheets, rolling them out like fresh pasta, and hanging them from cords that stretched the width of the room. She was surrounded by them. Translucent and mesmerizing, never quite dry, mostly fleshy colours but, where they caught the light that entered through the ceiling-high windows, they glowed like electric jellyfish. No one from the office disturbed Jacky as she worked amidst her subterranean laundry. They were afraid, as they always were, to approach her, although she imagined that her presence soothed them, perhaps even inspired them, the way the distant presence of her superiors had always motivated her.

She finished it at night. It was one in the morning, the rain pattered against the broad, high windows, raindrops illuminated by the streetlights below as they trickled down the glass. In the muted light of the city's flashes, Jacky birthed her offspring.

Breathless, she watched the patches of yellow and pink, beating with the electric pulse of a simulated heartbeat, a convulsive motion that sent a gust of air through the room. Like breath.

How to begin to describe this mutant child. It was imperfectly symmetrical. In isolation, each part was beautiful. Iridescent sheaths twitched with the electric current. It was thinner in places, stretched and on the verge of gaping where the metal frame and electric wires protruded and rose to the surface like bones and capillaries. It was a structure of contrasts between strong skeletal structures and that godly, glowing skin. It was all exactly as she'd imagined. It worked, as in, it was difficult to imagine the raw materials in any other configuration. Impossible, too, to imagine the events of her life any other way. Everything had led to this moment of creation. She was meant to make this inanimate body. She'd sacrificed family, friendships and belonging to create this home of flesh and bone. She had finally found her beetle's skin.

She was suddenly tired, more exhausted than she'd ever been. She couldn't go home, she couldn't move. She had to sleep. She crawled in through the opening of the structure, curling up deep inside of it. She trusted her dreams to keep her tethered to the womb she had birthed.

As she drifted, she thought she saw Mark, at the height of his love for her, paper in hand, folding his architectural origami. She kissed him, then flinched at the touch of cold limestone against her lips. His face had morphed into a statue of the jackal god. She watched the stone crumble, an avalanche of ashen bricks clouding her view. When the dust settled, her own body came into view. With a terrifying screech from nowhere, her ribcage parted, sucking her into a hollow darkness within, inverting, plummeting, dropping her on a sandy plane. She blinked and took in the barren landscape. Clarissa's body lay there, grave-worms crawling out through her wide-open mouth. Jacky shot awake.

It was light, the night had passed. The skin around her a warm, peachy hue. Shadows had appeared through the flesh filter. A humdrum of voices, a collective of bodies, radiating heat.

Jacky turned to her side, sweat coating her body, still soft from sleep. Holding her breath, she crawled towards the opening of her den. There was a flutter as she pushed her head through lips that framed the slit of the doorway, and fell into the white light of the journalists' camera flashes.

34

'I Have a Heart,' became the title of the viral video showing Jacky Mackenzie emerging from a womb-like contrap-
tion made of skin. The usually inexpressive, at most irritable,
woman was fraught with emotion as she appeared from her
fleshy fortress through the reconstruction of a vulva, belting
the words: 'See me, I'm alive. See me, I'm human. See me,
I have a heart!' She stood there, eyes wide, appealing to the
journalists she had invited into the architectural womb of
her firm's headquarters. She rotated her body, holding it flat
like a coin-face, catching the light of the cameras held by
the journalists who had gathered in a semi-circle around the
room, like her body was proof. The video was taken by most
as evidence of a psychological breakdown. It was difficult to
see it any other way. Her husband, it was widely known, had
filed for a divorce she refused to give. They had spent the best
part of two decades building a firm together. This separation
was a major rupture in both her personal and her professional life. This was a predictable response to an identity
in crisis. This was The Beetle's way – always efficient to the
point of apathetic. She was trying to recover herself through
her work. Only this time, she'd gone too far. This was the end.

The disdain of her critics, for the most part, turned to pity. Now that she was no longer dangerous. Although nobody knew exactly what kind of threat she'd posed.

Her ex-lover, though, couldn't afford such sentimentality. Besides, he knew better – that this display didn't represent the depths of breakdown but the height of pride. It was her pride, as far as he was concerned, that was the cause of her downfall. She refused to accept the terms of his ending. Had to do it her way. All for pride and at the cost of dignity.

He held his phone close to his face as he watched the video, as he had done most nights since it had infiltrated, then swarmed the internet. Jacky saying something about people not listening, not appreciating her. There was something strange about the tone of her voice. Something feeble, sunken, even doubtful. Mark pincered two fingers across the little screen, zooming in on her. Her hand was resting on that bulge of a bandage on her thigh. He moved back to her face, pale, head wavering, then back to her patent coat, which he realised was actually a blazer coated in some kind of goo. He released her from his digital hold and sighed.

Mark had gone for an evening walk to calm his nerves, as he had done most nights recently, in the charged interlude of static unrest in which he found himself. Entirely dependent on this strange woman he'd once known, to grant him access to a life after her. It was high summer in Sweden, endless daylight. Even now, at eleven at night, the sky was a bright shade of blue he'd discovered there. It was fluorescent, it brought out other colours he'd never imagined could belong to the natural world, leaves in the liquid greens of a child's paintbox.

He walked through the squelch of moist moss, through a field that surrounded his house. He'd chosen a house on the outskirts of Stockholm, that near-distance from the city was the one thing about the house with Jacky that had suited him well. He'd never made use of the space separating his house from the city back home, the green had served as a buffer, or a blockade. Now he saw it much less functionally.

He didn't agree with what the journalists were saying. His wife wasn't crazy, she was in the same liminal space he was. Mark knew that, despite appearances, it wasn't a bad place to be; it was a place of reinvention. Only they couldn't both reinvent themselves and stay upright. That impossibility revealed the limits of their dream. They couldn't really be streamlined together. One of them would always be the shadow blocking the other's light. In that nullifying construction only one of them could live. It was his turn.

Mark agreed to his lawyer's suggestion to leverage Jacky's well-documented residency inside her BeetleSkin. He agreed to build a case of insanity, to force her hand, and the divorce he needed. And so, he turned Jacky into the version of herself he needed her to be.

THE LAST VERSE

Acorn weevil
Curculio glandium
4-8mm

The acorn weevil is objectively bizarre. The entomologist does not use that adjective lightly. The beetle's most striking feature is a long snout, reminiscent of the nose of an anteater.

She uses this snout to bore into acorns, laying her eggs in the centre of the nut. Her larva feed on their container, until they are ready to tunnel out as fully grown adults.

Buried deep inside the tree's own offspring, a meeting of seeds is the start of this beetle's life. Cushioned by the corky padding of the acorn, she lives through the winter in the larval stage. When she emerges, she consumes the nut. She leaves the acorn's embryo intact, so that the plant, too, is free to reproduce itself. She is born in communion with another lifeform. Through a symbiosis of difference.

Jacky looked down at the gold on brown swivel patterns of an acorn weevil's skin, and suddenly saw her own capillaries.

What would it mean to be reborn from the inside of a nut? She wondered. To take her time to winter it out. To be born by choice, when she was ready. Perhaps she would find herself able to embrace the world's unknown, and the unknown of others. Perhaps, if she'd just been given the time, she'd have been able to take in the ingenious tools and the ingenious marks of others. To tunnel her way home with them. Alone, together.

35

Jacky needed to find a way out. She had been huddled in foetal position for a good twelve hours. She didn't know if it was part of the performance or if it just felt right.

Her birth had been anticlimactic, as births often are. Just the pelt of some ancestral memory of pain she had tried to leave behind. Maybe she would have been able to forget, if they'd let her. But she'd been met by the flash of cameras followed by more, relentless misinterpretations.

It was particularly hurtful this time because she'd been trying something so new. An entirely new hypothesis. She'd needed them to see it. She didn't need them to approve. As ever, she just needed someone to see it the way she intended. It was a basic human need, Clarissa would say, to be seen. Just another expression of our deeply social nature. We don't really exist until someone says our name, responds to our offering, touches our skin. With Mark gone, Jacky had been looking for her flash of recognition elsewhere. Confirmation that she belonged, at least broadly, to the same human species. But instead, she'd been confronted with her own strangeness. No one seemed to recognise her under-developed human heart for what it was. They saw a woman dislodged from reality, not one with her fingers on the pulse of existence. She'd failed to prove it to them, and so she'd failed to prove it to herself. Rebirth was a dead end. And so there was no escape.

She was huddled in the cushioning on the ground, soft and wet like a tongue. Covered in the same gooey glaze as the rest of her structure, she thought about her heart. She imagined it as a specimen on a plate for medical students to learn from. She thought of her heart all wet and stringy, of the severed aorta, blood congealed around the edges. Of the veins like the bulging vessels on a scrotum. Of the uncanny resemblance between all the human organs.

How had we arrived at these divisions? Who separated heart from guts or brain? Or birth from childhood, adolescence and old age? Who decided what we were, and what it all meant? Just people, in their attempts to contain what they didn't understand. People buried their noses deep in their answers, but that didn't stop them from dying. It didn't stop them from living either. That's what she found the most baffling. When Jacky took stock of her life and her attempts to contain it and sometimes end it, what struck her as the most remarkable observation was, that despite her worst efforts, she had survived. She was, as ever, condemned to another day. Sometimes, her attempts to come to a stand-still generated even more momentum. Life charging, like a windup toy, gearing up for more, meaningless motion. Once again, she was forced to commit to a course, however dissatisfying.

Life, like death, was a powerful thing.

The world was full of theories about existence. But she was now convinced, that she believed in science, and not religion. Religion told us that we succumbed because of our sins. But science had a better theory. Evolutionary theories, in particular, showed us how our mistakes made us. The task was not to overcome our sins, but to survive them. We were all mutants like the hydra, endings sprouting multiplying beginnings. And we had to live in those webs of our own making. Somehow, our hubris didn't destroy us, and that was terrifying. That, Jacky realised then, was where science and religion were truly opposed – in their evaluation of the human capacity to survive their own bullshit. Jacky, through her life's turns, was developing a distinctly scientific vision of hell.

Jacky wanted to learn, to grow, to develop, but everything in her environment seemed so indifferent. There was no encouragement, no recognition, there were no accolades and no monuments to her personal progress. There was just more, disinterested, life. But somehow, she had to go on living.

People put so much emphasis on the heart, she thought. They talked about the heart when they meant the brain. They'd stolen that symbol from the Egyptians, then made it the source of everything. Of emotion and wisdom, of memories and strength. They'd stuck with the ancient symbol because they thought it was beautiful. Jacky had resisted such empty aestheticism. But lying there in the cavity of her creature, she thought that perhaps it was, after all, missing a heart. That if she just let herself have one, perhaps it wouldn't make for such a bad symbol after all.

She didn't really have a choice. It was between staying huddled there in the eternal limbo of her woman-sized amniotic sac, or trying something new. If there was a perfect option, there wouldn't be a choice. As long as there were decisions to make, there would be trial and error. Thesis, and antithesis. Different Jackys, different skins. Maybe that's why people liked the heart so much, with its truthful dialectics, a beat is a beat is a beat.

36

'Imagine we're old and all the choices that made our lives seem inevitable.'

Jacky stood on Clarissa's doorstep. She hadn't brought anything with her, but she wanted to come in.

It had been months since the video. Clarissa hadn't heard from Jacky throughout her absurd performance. Nor had she been told the insignificant detail that Mark had filed for divorce. She'd had to find out from stupid articles. Because Jacky had decided she wasn't worth telling. Thought it wasn't worth informing the woman who had been at her beck-and-call throughout that tumultuous marriage, that it had come to its predictably explosive end.

Clarissa stood blocking the doorway, arms folded, unimpressed.

'Who chose who and how or even why won't matter, because our life together will be indisputable.'

Jacky had spent the past thirty minutes trying to convince Clarissa that she was a changed woman. That she was definitively choosing to be with her. Not as a last resort, but because everything she had ever done had led her here. When that didn't work, she'd tried a different tack.

'And we'll have permission. To stop making choices. All we'll have to do, is accept our lives as they were.'

'I never needed permission.'

'I know you didn't. You've always seen that. But I see it now. That you don't actually have to be old to be allowed to be slow and pointless.'

Clarissa stifled a smile. It was a novelty, watching Jacky try to be romantic. A once-in-a-lifetime serenade.

Clarissa liked what Jacky was saying, of course she did. But she had to give some credence to the doubts she'd felt over the months of neglect. From the outside, the series of events made her look like a last resort. It was everything she'd expected. Just as painful, too. Jacky's husband had left her and now she'd come knocking at her door. It was the predetermined outcome. The events were fixed, but it suddenly occurred to her, that their meaning didn't have to be. Jacky made her see that.

As ever, Jacky also had an alternative explanation of the same reality. Jacky told her the marriage had to break for her to be able to commit herself fully to Clarissa. It was a process, 'a natural cycle,' she said, of 'decay and germination'. She always talked about plants when she was trying to be convincing.

Clarissa had to admit that it wasn't hard to see why Jacky had thought it would bring Clarissa some relief, to see that glass prison of a marriage smashed to pieces. Clarissa had wondered sometimes whether she'd been too openly disapproving of Mark. It was a form of betrayal, a breaching of the terms of their open relationship. She was supposed to accept Jacky's choices. But she'd taken a firm stance in the spirit of that other, silent pact, they had: to be Jacky's harbour, to be the point of truth to return to. And she'd kept that commitment, at least. She'd never lied to Jacky about what she deserved.

'Imagine we're at the end of our lives, and time is running out, and taking stock is pointless. We're just thinking of what's next. And we're sitting in the sand, if we can find a patch of beach without pebbles, and we're looking out over the ocean. And we're holding hands, and our skin is all salty and freckled and falling off our bones like—' Jacky paused, looking for the appropriate word, 'like droopy ham.' Clarissa smirked again, she couldn't help herself, at Jacky's version of romance, its morbidly clinical flair. 'And we fold our skin together and hold tight, and we brace ourselves. I don't think there's anything more terrifying and I want to experience it with you. Not because I'm scared to do it alone, but because I think there'll be more to it if we do it together.'

Clarissa didn't really believe Jacky had been reborn, but the idea of it did give her a way out of the closed circuit she and Mark had built. If Jacky had been reborn, perhaps that freed her, and them all, from the roles they had played. Perhaps Jacky had been born to a fresh slate where she loved Clarissa not because she needed someone, but because she wanted her, and where Clarissa wasn't a choice relative to Mark, but someone worth choosing in her own right. She was surprised, and impressed that Jacky had found her a loophole, but then she remembered that structures were Jacky's life, and so of course she'd been able to build one that suited them better. She just had to want to.

A universal human defence mechanism. Clarissa stared at Jacky, who didn't look as small as she should have done, down there on the pavement looking up at her. Clarissa could see their opening now, but she still couldn't bring herself to pull Jacky in. Now that Jacky was a real possibility, she wasn't sure about any of it. So she did what she always did, and reframed her own vulnerabilities in universal terms, to give her the strength to push through.

Jacky stared down at the cracked slate slabs between them.

'It's not like I ever didn't choose you.'

'You've not chosen me every day for a decade.'

'I'm sorry.'

Coming from Jacky, those words were full of potential.

'You don't have to say that,' Clarissa said. She wasn't sure if she meant that Jacky didn't have to be sorry or if that there was no point apologising, because there would always be more to be sorry for. But they both knew it was the kind of ambiguity they needed to start again.

37

Jacky didn't change overnight. Clarissa wouldn't have expected that, she was more realistic about that than Jacky could have been. She knew that a part of Jacky, or a version of Jacky, would return to her web of thoughts that tied her to her past with Mark. That she would tug at those threads, testing theories about what could have been. She was right. With Clarissa, Jacky was discovering what real stability was. It was changing her, massaging her into something less inflexible. She regretted never having shared that side of herself with Mark. The side that would have softened if they'd let it. She wondered what would have become of them if she had. But maybe, she thought, it took that relationship breaking for her to see that. And so she'd come full circle. She didn't regret what they'd had. They'd had their definitions, and those had got them far. Definitions had helped them build their house, only in the end that house was built not for dwelling, but for metamorphosis.

Jacky would continue to rehearse that loop. It helped her stay put as she wandered. Usually at night. After Clarissa had disappeared hazily to bed, Jacky would walk along the suburban streets of her new life, down to the beach front. It was a side of the ocean she liked to see. A Saturday-night warzone of barely-dressed adolescents vomiting on the steps of beachfront hotels. Girls in spandex tube dresses, floored, heeled legs jutting out like harpoons. Jacky liked to watch the colourful carnage ooze down the concrete walkway, the bursts of neon yellow and glitter and leather and fur. It soothed her to watch drunkenness give way to dawn, revealing the night's delusions. To watch people awaken to their mortality. Clothes turning from armour to costumes. Understanding that it had all just been a touch of alien sparkle transporting them for a few hours in the dark. They wouldn't fully sober up, of course, until kebab meat slid down the back of their tongues and lined the insides of their stomachs. Only the touch of another being's flesh would give them the carnal strength they needed to face the truth. Jacky liked to watch those people. She needed them to remind her how they were all connected by their imagination. They helped her dull her phantom fight or flight instinct.

She stayed put as she wandered. Sometimes she imagined going back. Back to smash the glass house to pieces. She imagined the glass walls hot, baked to the point of bursting. She coaxed herself to that shrill second before she let it fade. She imagined what the journalists would say. Or the thousands of people who had watched her on the screens of their phones. Through intact lenses that they believed showed them everything they needed to know. She knew the kinds of stories they told. Like the story of the power-hungry beetle, and the mortal man who was a little more like them. In the glowing lights of their digital oracles, the artificial flickers would reassure them. That this crabby and impersonable woman, with her darkness and her light – that tiring complexity – was nothing. Just a displaceable apparition. They'd decide that they could be jackals too, and condemn the heartless woman to the depths of a place destined for pointless people. The people who broke down dreams into unfamiliar pieces, then built them into stranger things, only to smash them to bits all over again. The people who broke so that they could go on pretending they couldn't.

She imagined smashing the house to pieces. But she didn't do it. It wasn't their voices that stopped her. It was because imagining it was enough. It was enough to picture herself in the aftermath, amidst the shards of glass jutting from the ground, life sprouting relentlessly around her. To look up, along with that version of herself, at the open sky, knowing that life wouldn't stop. To picture how nature would find its way into her body. Fungus followed by moss. How someday a foot would hit the mound of her corpse, covered in grass, and a face would turn towards it, smile, and think it was beautiful. It was enough to imagine impossible things, while letting herself live a possible life. That didn't make the impossible any less real, nor the possible any less important. Because there was no way out.

It was just such an adjustment, living without the mirror of faces and their confusing versions of her. It would take time, to turn her gaze from the reflections in her fishbowl. To look to the ocean instead, where boats sail one day and sink the next, where lost souls sweep the beds with the undulating tides, and where she was always full.

38

Clarissa brought the boat. Small, delicate, just a model. She'd made it with the mother who had lost her son. Clarissa had brought it to the memorial the boy's mother had organised for him. She didn't have to ask Jacky to come. On their way to the beach, Jacky remembered how, a year ago, she too, had built a model in the hope that it would bring her back to life. She recognised that same longing in the eyes of the mother. Jacky had tried to imagine what the mother would look like. She'd pictured her soft-spoken, all pastels and pies. She was nothing like it. She wore khaki trousers and combat boots. She spoke in spacious monosyllables that told you everything you needed to know. She wore her hair the way most of Clarissa's friends did, salty strands tied in a loose knot. There was a big crowd on the beach but Clarissa had managed to get them a spot at the front – somehow, without pushing, her openness always opening life up for the both of them. When the mother arrived, Clarissa handed her the boat. She held it in her hands, taking a breath before she dared to look down at it, eyes blurring, then, suddenly, clear.

'It's good,' she said.

Jacky looked at Clarissa, who nodded quietly.

There were no speeches. There was nothing to say. There was no story to tell. The boy was there, then he was gone. There was no reason for it. There was no consolation. All there was to do was to turn to the ocean, and share the silence. The hundred, maybe more, friends and locals gathered there, all turned to the waves, taking comfort in the way that glass burst into froth. The mother removed her boots. She left them by Clarissa's feet and walked barefoot into the ocean, carrying the boat. Jacky watched her along with the others, all resisting the urge to join her, gifting her the sea.

Jacky wondered if it felt as good to everyone else, to feel the thumping of their heart against their ribcage as they watched the mother walk away. Whether it helped them too, to imagine it was the boy, curled up inside of her, punching to break free. To pretend that it was them, and not nothingness, holding him captive. She wondered if it was a common human experience to prefer guilt over complexity. She still grappled with these questions, still worried, in moments, that she had a scarab where the heart should be.

A wailing passed through the crowd. It began as inarticulate rumblings, then, as it moved deeper into the crowd, grew into a song. Jacky tried to listen, but she found it easier to tune into the cracks in Clarissa's voice. That was less overwhelming to her.

Clarissa looked at her. They smiled at each other, sharing quiet tears. The mother was knee-deep in the waves now. She held the boat close to the water's surface, let it hover there. A moment passed, as she let the stream of water pass under it. Clarissa squeezed Jacky's hand, before the boat hit the water's surface and disappeared instantly, guzzled up by the waves. The mother looked almost embarrassed, like she'd failed to give the crowd the swansong they'd come for. As if she'd wanted to give them the chance she'd never had.

They stood and watched until the wind picked up, drowning out their wails. Then they all turned to go home, to sleep deeply the way you have to after facing death. Jacky and Clarissa walked back, in silence for a while. With her hand wrapped inside Clarissa's, Jacky imagined their faces ageing, in bursts, like a timelapse. After a while, Clarissa began to talk. She told Jacky about her sessions with the mother. How in the wake of trauma, the woman had been unable to speak, how after a while she'd found movement in her hands, then some words. How, finally, they'd made something.

ACKNOWLEDGEMENTS

As ever, I want to thank my agent, Eli Keren, and my publisher, the mighty Dead Ink, for believing in my weird little stories.

I also want to thank my family, friends, and Luong for supporting me through the creative storms, and everything in between. Your support makes the words on the page both less defining, and more meaningful.

A special thanks to Bruce, for being my first reader on this one. Our stories are entwined, and we both have so many to tell. I hope we'll stay connected in both senses.

ABOUT THE AUTHOR

Marieke Bigg is the author of *Waiting for Ted*, and *This Won't Hurt*. Writing across fiction and non-fiction, she deconstructs the cultural givens around bodies, minds, and identity. She holds a PhD in Sociology from the University of Cambridge, where she studied the technological transformation of human reproduction. She now lives in London. In addition to her books, Marieke speaks about the sociology of medicine and psychiatry, and collaborates with biologists and artists to explore the social potential of science. She is also a training psychotherapist.

About Dead Ink

Dead Ink is a publisher of bold new fiction based in Liverpool. We're an Arts Council England National Portfolio Organisation.

If you would like to keep up to date with what we're up to, check out our website and join our mailing list.

www.deadinkbooks.com | @deadinkbooks